"I'm sure there are plenty of women who'd like to get to know you."

Alex expelled a resigned breath. "Really. Why? So that they could say they'd seen the spot where the dastardly deed took place?"

"No." Kate sensed that, despite his mockery, it still hurt him to talk about it. "Are you telling me you haven't brought any other women to—to the house since your wife died?"

Alex's eyes narrowed. "I don't think that's anything to do with you, Mrs. Hughes," he responded harshly. "Are you sure you're not working for someone else as well as me?"

Kate went cold. "I don't know what you mean."

"I mean my father-in-law. Perhaps he can't get the answers he wants from my staff, so he's sent you."

"I can assure yo⸻

Kate managed ⸻
feeling. For a m⸻
he'd guessed w⸻

ANNE MATHER has been writing since she was seven, but it was only when her first child was born that she fulfilled her dream of becoming a published author. Since then, Anne has written more than 130 novels, reaching a readership that spans the world.

Born and raised in the north of England, Anne still makes her home there with her husband, two children and, now, grandchildren. Asked if she finds writing a lonely occupation, she replies that her characters always keep her company. In fact, she is so busy sorting out their lives that she often doesn't have time for her own! An avid reader herself, she devours everything from sagas and romances to suspense.

Books by Anne Mather

HARLEQUIN PRESENTS®
1947—DISHONOURABLE INTENT
1959—SINFUL PLEASURES
2000—MORGAN'S CHILD
2019—PACIFIC HEAT

Also available in MIRA® Books
DANGEROUS TEMPTATION

ANNE MATHER

Her Guilty Secret

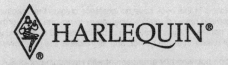

TORONTO • NEW YORK • LONDON
AMSTERDAM • PARIS • SYDNEY • HAMBURG
STOCKHOLM • ATHENS • TOKYO • MILAN • MADRID
PRAGUE • WARSAW • BUDAPEST • AUCKLAND

ISBN 0-373-12032-X

HER GUILTY SECRET

First North American Publication 1999.

CHAPTER ONE

THE man sitting at the other side of the desk cleared his throat. 'You are familiar with this kind of thing, aren't you?' he asked, glancing doubtfully about the office. Kate guessed that her addition of some pot plants and a parlour palm had caught his eye. Perhaps they didn't look very professional, she thought defensively, but they brightened up what was otherwise a rather gloomy room.

'Perfectly familiar,' she answered him now, shuffling the papers in front of her as if each and every one of them was a case pending her attention. In fact, since her father's death, the cases had been few and far between. Not everyone was prepared to trust their secrets to a woman who looked considerably younger than her thirty-two years. And the name on the door said William Ross, Private Investigator, which meant they were already disappointed when they encountered a woman instead. 'Just give me the details of the last time you saw your wife, and I'll do my best to get you a satisfactory result.'

The man hesitated, evidently still not convinced she could handle the matter, and Kate fought back the urge to scream. For heaven's sake, she thought, what was so difficult about finding a missing spouse? Her father used to practically survive on such cases, usually finding the runaway in some other man's bed.

'You do understand this must be dealt with in the strictest confidence?' he persisted, and Kate gave him her most convincing look. But she couldn't help the thought that he was not the most appealing of clients. He was wearing a worn jacket and trousers and grubby trainers, and she had to wonder if he could afford her services.

'Any information you give me is totally confidential,' she assured him firmly, aware of a certain reluctance to take on this case. But beggars can't be choosers, she reminded herself dryly, and her mother wouldn't be very pleased if she started turning clients away.

'The charges,' he said now, as if putting off the moment when he had to give her his wife's details. 'Are they negotiable?'

'I'm afraid not.' Kate always hated this part of the business. 'It's a hundred pounds a day, plus expenses. And I'm afraid I have to ask for payment in advance.'

'In advance?' His rather close-set eyes widened in a face that was neither distinguished nor memorable. Kate imagined he was in his late forties, but the downward curve of his mouth added at least half a dozen more years.

'It's customary,' she said, endeavouring to sound professional. 'After all, if I have no luck in finding your wife, you might object to paying then. Besides—' she forced a smile '—naturally there are expenses. But I'll keep a record of what I spend on a day-to-day basis.'

'Hmm.' The man considered her explanation with a drawn brow, and Kate began to feel uncomfortable. If she'd had only herself to care about, she'd have been quite happy to send him on his way. To some other agency, with a man to attend to his needs.

But she wasn't a free agent. And, despite the law degree that she'd spent more years than she cared to remember getting, this was the only job she had. Of course, if she'd been prepared to move to London, she might have been able to find some solicitor willing to give her a chance. But in a small town like King's Montford there were too many articled clerks already waiting for dead men's shoes.

The man was fumbling in his jacket pocket now, pulling out an envelope that looked surprisingly thick. Opening the flap, he threw a wad of notes on the desk in front of her. 'Will that do to be going on with?' he asked. 'There's a couple of thousand there.'

Kate tried not to look as shocked as she felt. Most of the clients she'd had recently had been prepared to put up a couple of days' expenses and nothing more. What couldn't she do with two thousand pounds? she thought weakly. She could pay the rent, for one thing, and give Joanne the money she needed for that school skiing trip.

'I—that's fine,' she said now, inadequately, though she held back from picking up the notes. Her father's training was warning her to find out what the job entailed before she committed herself. Even if she couldn't see any immediate problem in attempting to locate his wife.

'Good.' The man, who had been resting one foot on his knee, now dropped it to the floor and leaned forward in his chair. 'I expect you want to know her name, don't you?' he said. 'And the last time I saw her.'

'It would help,' said Kate whimsically, but then, seeing no answering humour in his expression, she quickly sobered. She mustn't let him know that this contribution to her finances had brought her such a sense of relief. And she hadn't decided to take the job yet, she reminded herself. What had her father always told her? Make sure it was legal first.

'All right.' The man nodded. 'Her name's Sawyer; Alicia Sawyer.'

'Alicia—Sawyer.' Kate grabbed a clean pad and wrote the woman's name at the top. But Alicia, she thought ruefully. Somehow that name didn't go with the rather shifty individual sitting opposite. Still—

'She hasn't been seen for a couple of months,' he added, rather curiously, Kate thought. Had he waited two months before deciding to report her missing? Or had the police been dealing with the matter up till now?

'And your name, Mr Sawyer?' she ventured, deciding to take things in order. 'Your first name, that is,' she appended, arching her dark brows. 'Just for my records, of course.'

He frowned. 'Is that necessary?'

'If you don't mind.'

He waited a beat. 'It's—Henry,' he said at last. 'Henry Sawyer,' he repeated, with a sniff. 'Can we get on?'

Kate wrote his name beside that of his wife and then looked up. 'Of course,' she said pleasantly. 'Perhaps you'd better start by giving me her description. Or do you have a photograph?'

'What? Oh—yeah.' He rifled his pockets again and came up with a two-by-four-inch snapshot. 'That do?' he asked, hunching his shoulders with obvious irritation.

Kate looked at the photograph. She saw a blonde-haired woman with a well-developed figure. The photograph was slightly smudged so the finer details were not clearly defined. 'Um—how old is Mrs Sawyer?' she asked, frowning, surprised at how attractive the woman was.

'I—' He hesitated and then blew out a breath. 'Thirty-nine,' he volunteered shortly. 'Yeah, that's right. Thirty-nine.'

Kate nodded and added that detail to her pad. 'I assume you reported her disappearance to the police?'

He looked down at his hands. 'Yeah, yeah,' he said. 'Of course I told the police my suspicions. But you know what?' He looked up. 'They didn't want to know.'

Kate stared at him. 'I find that hard to believe.'

'Oh, they went through the motions,' he muttered harshly. 'But I didn't have any real evidence. That was when I knew that finding her was up to me.'

Kate was confused. 'You say you reported your wife's disappearance to the police and they did nothing about it?'

He shrugged. 'Sort of.' And then, seeing her incredulity, he said, 'That's right.'

'But—'

'See, she wasn't living with me when she disappeared,' he added abruptly, and Kate began to get the feeling that he was just wasting her time.

'Not living with you?'

'No.' Sawyer flashed her a look of dislike. 'She walked

out six months ago. Women!' He scowled. 'The bitch didn't even leave me a note.'

The bitch!

Kate made another note on her pad and then slid another sheet of paper over it. She didn't want him to see what she'd written down. 'If your wife left you six months ago—'

'She did.'

'Then surely her whereabouts are not your problem. If she doesn't want you to know where she is, Mr Sawyer—'

'I know where she went,' he broke in savagely, and Kate felt an uneasy twinge of alarm. She was alone in the building, the other office workers having left for home over an hour ago. She'd even let Susie go, assuring her she could manage on her own. She'd only hung on because Sawyer had asked her to. He'd maintained he couldn't make it before six o'clock.

'If you know—' she began faintly, remembering that her father's old revolver was still in the bottom drawer of the desk. If he made a move on her, she could always threaten to use it. She didn't know if it was loaded, of course, but he wouldn't know that.

'Until she disappeared, I knew exactly where she was living,' he informed her impatiently, but at least he seemed less aggressive than before. 'But, like I said, no one's seen her recently, and I want to know where she is, all right?'

'All right.' Kate sighed, wondering how to broach her next question. 'Would you like to tell me why she—walked out?'

'Why d'you think? That bastard seduced her into leaving me, didn't he?' His jaw compressed. 'He stole my wife, Mrs Ross. And now she's disappeared, and he won't say where she's gone.'

Kate didn't correct him. Although her name wasn't Ross, it was sometimes easier to let people think it was. It gave a certain anonymity to her private life, and enabled her to use her own name when she didn't want to advertise her occupation.

She frowned. It was all becoming abundantly clear. This

woman, his wife, Alicia Sawyer—that name still stuck in her throat—had run off with a man her husband knew. A friend of his, perhaps? But no longer, obviously. If that was the case, she saw no reason why she shouldn't take it on.

'The other man,' she ventured now. 'You know him?'

'Oh, yeah, I know him,' he snarled, baring nicotine-stained teeth. 'His name's Kellerman; Alex Kellerman. Have you heard of him? He owns that big property just off the Bath Road.'

Kate felt her jaw drop and quickly rescued it. It wouldn't do to let her client see how shocked she was. But Alex Kellerman, she thought incredulously. She couldn't believe it. What would a man like Kellerman want with Henry Sawyer's wife?

But she had no right to think that way, she chided herself severely. If her photograph was anything to go by, Alicia Sawyer was a beautiful woman, and any man would be proud to be seen with her. Just because Alex Kellerman had had his own problems, that did not mean he was immune to sexual attraction. Life was full of surprises. She should know; her own life hadn't exactly gone to plan.

'I—know who Mr Kellerman is,' she said now. And then, just in case he took her words literally, she added, 'I mean, I've heard of him, of course.' She tapped her pen against the pad in front of her, suddenly aware of the ramifications. 'The Kellerman stables are well known in King's Montford.' She took a breath. 'Um—how did your wife meet Mr Kellerman? Do you know?'

Sawyer gave her another scornful stare. 'Of course I know!' he exclaimed, as if it should have been obvious to her as well. 'She worked for him, didn't she?'

'Did she?' Kate's dark brows ascended again, but she refused to be intimidated this time. 'Well...' She made another note on her pad. 'That explains a lot. In what capacity was she employed?'

Sawyer regarded her sourly. 'You mean what was the job he offered her, don't you?' Kate nodded and he rubbed his nose with a grimy finger. 'Some kind of office work, I think. That's what she told me, anyway.'

'Right.' Kate added that piece of information to her list. 'Did she work there long?'

'Long enough.' Sawyer was bitter. 'Long enough to persuade her to leave me. We were happy enough until she went to work at Jamaica Hill.'

'And where did she go when she left you?' Kate thought she could see where this was going, but she wanted him to lay it out.

'To Jamaica Hill, of course. She went to live with Kellerman. She moved in there about six months ago.'

'Ah.' Kate rolled her lips inward. 'And you believe they were having an affair?'

'I don't just believe it. I know it.' He grimaced. 'She left me, didn't she? Why else would she do that?'

Kate could think of several reasons but she didn't voice them. 'And now you say she's not there any more.'

'She's gone missing,' he corrected her, his tone sour. 'I— I loved the silly bitch, didn't I? I've kept tabs on her ever since she left.'

Kate wondered if that constituted stalking, and then put the thought out of her head. It wasn't up to her to question his motives. If his wife had disappeared, it surely couldn't be too difficult to find out where she'd gone.

'So—you'd like to know where she's working now,' she said carefully, refusing to give any credit to a more sinister solution. He was jealous and resentful. That was normal. It was quite a relief to understand where he was coming from.

'If she is working somewhere else,' he put in grimly, and she couldn't quite suppress the unease that his words aroused inside her. 'See, she disappeared more than eight weeks ago. And no one seems to have heard from her since.'

Kate swallowed. 'She's probably left King's Montford,' she said, ignoring her misgivings. 'Perhaps she doesn't want—anyone—to know where she's gone.'

'I don't believe that,' he contradicted her harshly. 'That

bastard's hiding something. And I guess you remember what happened to Kellerman's wife.'

Kate sucked in a breath. 'You're not seriously suggesting—'

'That he killed her?' interrupted Sawyer disparagingly. 'Why not? He got away with it before, didn't he?'

Kate gasped. 'Mrs Kellerman's death was accidental.'

'Was it?'

'Of course.' But she could feel herself trembling, even so. 'Besides,' she persevered, 'Mrs Sawyer was an employee. If he'd wanted to get rid of her, he only had to fire her.'

Sawyer could see her indecision. 'And what if Alicia refused to go quietly? Who knows what kind of scandal that would have caused? She was a sucker for a clever line, but she could be awkward, if it suited her. I doubt if Kellerman's business could have survived any more bad publicity.'

Kate shook her head. What had begun—in her eyes, at least—as a simple inquiry had suddenly assumed the proportions of a major investigation. Or it had if she gave any credence to what he was implying. For God's sake, was he mad? Alex Kellerman was not a monster. His wife had died in suspicious circumstances, but he'd been absolved of any blame.

And yet...

She didn't want to consider it, but she couldn't help remembering the torrid headlines a couple of years ago when Pamela Kellerman had broken her neck. She'd apparently been riding a horse that her husband knew to be dangerous, the tabloids had reported. At a time when she was three months pregnant with the couple's second child.

There'd been a lot of speculation, she recalled reluctantly. Despite Pamela Kellerman's pregnancy, it had been common knowledge that Alex Kellerman and his wife were having marital problems. It had been mooted that it was only because of their daughter, who had been two years old at the time, that they'd stayed together. It had even been hinted that the child she'd been carrying when she fell to her death wasn't her husband's. That she'd been having an affair and that was why her husband had snapped.

Of course, it had all been speculation. And the newspapers had been careful not to print anything that might give Alex Kellerman a reason to sue. But the fact remained that Pamela Kellerman should not have been riding that particular horse, and no one had ever satisfactorily explained why two horses with similar markings—but very dissimilar temperaments—should have been put into opposite stalls.

The inquest had proved to be quite a drama, with Pamela's father accusing his son-in-law in court. He had had to be led away by his solicitor, she remembered. Alex Kellerman had been cold and tight-lipped throughout the whole proceedings, but there'd been no evidence to implicate him. Pamela's death had been judged accidental, and although the rumours had persisted for some time they'd eventually died away.

Recalling Alex Kellerman's hard, yet compelling features—as portrayed in the newspaper reports at the time—Kate couldn't dispel a shiver of apprehension. But she couldn't allow Sawyer to go around making accusations he couldn't prove. 'Mrs Kellerman's death was an accident,' she insisted firmly. 'I'm not surprised the police didn't take you seriously if you made unsubstantiated allegations like that.'

'You said anything I told you would be treated as confidential,' he reminded her sharply. 'Now, do you want the job or not? I don't have time to f—to mess around.'

Kate made a pretence of studying her notes to give herself time to consider. Were her rent and Joanne's school trip really worth the hassle of taking this case? So far all she'd handled were divorce and insurance investigations. She was making a living, but only just.

And, if she ignored her client's surely exaggerated insinuations, it should be a fairly straightforward inquiry. Alicia Sawyer had worked for Alex Kellerman for some time so there would obviously be people at the stables who remembered her. It ought to be easy enough to find out why she'd left and where she'd gone. If they'd known who Sawyer was—and that seemed likely—they'd probably been reluctant to divulge any information to him.

'I'll need a few more details,' she said at last, hoping she wasn't going to regret her decision. 'When did you first suspect that Alex Kellerman was interested in your wife? Have you spoken to her since she left? And did she take all her belongings with her?'

It was after eight o'clock when Kate let herself into the apartment she shared with her mother and daughter in Milner Court. It had been dark and cold as she drove her father's old Vauxhall through the empty streets of King's Montford, but the apartment was warm and welcoming, and the living room, where her mother and twelve-year-old Joanne were watching television, was cosy in the lamplight.

'You're late!' exclaimed her mother at once, getting to her feet and coming across the room to meet her. 'I put your supper in the oven a couple of hours ago, so I doubt if it's very palatable now.'

'Don't worry. I had a sandwich in lieu of lunch at about three o'clock so I'm not particularly hungry,' replied Kate, smiling as her daughter raised a languid hand in her direction. 'Hi, darling,' she added. 'I hope you did your homework before you started watching the box.'

'I did,' said Joanne placidly, and her grandmother confirmed it with a nod.

'She did it before supper. When you said you'd be late, we hung on for you. For a while, anyway. I didn't think you meant half-past eight.'

'I didn't,' admitted Kate ruefully, taking off her overcoat. 'But my client was late, and after he'd gone I called into the *Herald's* office to do some initial checking into the facts of the case. I should have rung, I know, but I didn't expect to take so long. I'm sorry if you've been worried.'

'So you should be,' agreed her mother wryly, removing Kate's overcoat from the back of the chair where she'd deposited it and folding it over her arm to hang away. 'I assume Susie was with you, was she?'

'Well, no.' Kate was contrite. 'She had a hot date tonight, so I said she could go.' Besides, Susie was a teenager. She answered phones and did some necessary typing, but that was all.

Mrs Ross shook her head. 'Well, I think you're very foolish. You know how I feel about you seeing clients after hours. Your father was a man. He could look after himself.'

'I can look after myself, too,' Kate insisted, pulling a face. 'Honestly, Mum, you're so sexist at times.'

'But realistic,' remarked Joanne, turning from the soap she was watching to give her mother a warning look. 'Come on, Mum, we both know your martial arts training wouldn't be much good against a knife. Get real! You're no match for a serious villain.'

'I don't deal with serious villains,' retorted her mother impatiently, her eyes darting a silent plea for restraint. Joanne knew how her grandmother worried. Didn't she have any more sense than to suggest she was running a risk? 'You've been watching too much television,' she added. 'My cases are very ordinary, as you know.'

'So far,' said Joanne, ignoring her mother's expression and determined to have the last word. 'So who is this man you had to see after hours? Was he ordinary, too?'

Kate thought guiltily of the two thousands pounds residing in her shoulder bag and then pushed the memory aside. 'Very ordinary,' she said determinedly. 'And you know I never discuss my cases with you.'

It wasn't until she was safely in bed that Kate allowed herself to think about the case again. She was still not at all sure she had made the right decision in accepting it, and she tucked the covers beneath her chin as if to ward off the sudden sense of chill that invaded her bones.

Yet, she had only Henry Sawyer's word that Alicia Sawyer had disappeared, and the idea that there might be something suspicious about it if she had was purely supposition. Her client hardly inspired confidence, and with a husband like him Alicia might just be keeping out of his way.

She'd probably moved on, got another job, decided not to let her husband know where she was going. Kate didn't believe for a moment that Alex Kellerman was involved in her disappearance. It was far too melodramatic and smacked of a desire for revenge rather than justice.

If—and she had no real proof of this yet—if Alicia had had a relationship with Alex Kellerman, what of it? There was no law that said a man shouldn't have an affair with an employee. The only unpleasant aspect of the situation was that he'd taken another woman to live in the house which he'd shared with Pamela. He must have known it would cause gossip—or didn't he care?

The Kellermans had only been married for three years when she'd fallen to her death. Kate had discovered that that evening during the time she'd spent going over the old news reports. She'd also learned that his daughter had only narrowly avoided witnessing the accident. Kate's heart ached for the little girl and the trauma she must have suffered since.

She sighed. Not for the first time, she wished her father was still alive so that she could have discussed her thoughts with him. She'd have welcomed his advice. His experience had meant a lot. The tragedy was, they'd only worked together for a few months before he'd had the heart attack that had killed him. A heart attack, her mother was convinced, which had been brought on by the strains of the job.

But she'd have been grateful for his wisdom now, thought Kate ruefully. The wisdom of any man, she conceded, aware that her own life was sadly lacking in that department. But since Sean had been killed she'd shied away from any serious attachment, and despite the fact that it was over ten years since his death she rarely admitted a man into her life.

In the beginning, she'd made Joanne the excuse, and it was true that immediately after the accident she had clung to her small daughter. She'd been bitter then, and hurt. She'd given up so much for Sean Hughes, and, however devastated she'd felt when he was killed, he had let her down.

Her parents had been marvellous, of course. Despite the fact that they'd never approved of her relationship with Sean, they'd been there when she needed them. They'd given her and Joanne a home when the house she'd shared with Sean had had to be sold, and they'd supported her until she could get a job and get back on her feet.

She punched her pillow, trying to get comfortable, but thoughts of her husband's betrayal only added to the restlessness she was feeling tonight. It was listening to Henry Sawyer describe his wife's infidelities. It had reminded her of so much she wanted to forget...

She'd been in her freshman year at university when she'd first met Sean. She'd been working at the supermarket during the Easter holidays, stacking shelves, trying to make some money to supplement her grant, when he'd started taking an interest in her. It had been such a thrill, she remembered unwillingly. All the other girls had been fascinated by the handsome young under-manager and she wouldn't have been human if she hadn't been flattered by his attention.

They'd started a relationship: a light-hearted one to begin with, but by Christmas it was getting really heavy. He'd wanted her to stay in King's Montford, not to go back to Warwick in January, to move in with him instead. He was crazy about her, he'd told her, and he didn't know what he'd do if she left him now.

What he'd really meant, Kate had realised, was that if she went back to university he wouldn't wait for her. There'd be some other woman by the time she came back in the summer. And, because she'd thought she was in love with him, she'd abandoned her law degree, marrying him instead and moving into the tiny house he owned in Queen Street, and staying on at the supermarket full-time.

They'd been happy, for a while anyway. Even her parents, who had been so disappointed by her decision to give up her university place, had swallowed their pride and helped them to buy a car. When Joanne had come along, they'd been delighted to welcome their granddaughter, even if they would have preferred for Kate and Sean to have saved some money before they'd brought a baby into the world.

Then, a few days before Joanne's second birthday, Kate's world had fallen apart. Sean had told Kate he was going to Bristol on business, but when the police had come to give her the terrible news about the accident they'd been forced to tell her there'd been a woman with him in the car. They'd both been killed instantly when the Sierra had run into the back of a stationary wagon that had been parked on the hard shoulder, and Kate had been left to speculate what Sean had been doing to swerve so badly off the road.

At the inquest, she'd learned that they'd both been drinking, and, in the absence of any other evidence, a verdict of death while under the influence of alcohol had been returned. She'd learned later, from a well-meaning sympathiser, that Sean had been having an affair with the woman who'd died with him. It had been a long-term relationship by all accounts, which had started when she was pregnant with Joanne.

She'd realised then that she'd had her suspicions all along. Sean had been absent too many times for all his excuses of overtime to be true. She'd been burying her head for so long, it had been hard to come to terms with it and many more months had passed before she was able to face the future with any optimism.

Not that she regretted all of what had happened. Her daughter was a constant source of delight to her. But when Joanne was six Kate had known she had to get on with her life. She'd enrolled at Bristol University and finished the degree she'd started at Warwick, which enabled her to travel to college every day but come home every night to put Joanne to bed.

However, when she'd eventually tried to get a job, she'd found it wasn't that easy. There were few jobs around, and no one wanted to employ a thirty-year-old unmarried mother when there were plenty of younger, unencumbered graduates around. After months without success, her father had offered a temporary solution. He needed an assistant, he'd said, now that his secretary had retired, and Kate's legal training would come in very useful.

She'd thought he was only being kind to begin with, that, far from needing another assistant, there was barely enough work for one. But, gradually, she'd come to realise that she did have her uses, that she could do all the legwork while her father concentrated his talents in solving the cases.

They'd been a good team, too, she reflected, a lump forming in her throat. And she'd become interested in the business, and eager to learn all she could. But then her father had had his fatal heart attack and word had got around that Kate was on her own, and for a while the jobs had just stopped coming. She'd been half afraid she'd have to find something else to do.

But, slowly, she was gaining people's confidence, and because she'd had several successful results the business was coming back. Which was why she hadn't hesitated when Sawyer had asked her to see him after hours. She couldn't afford to give a negative response.

Yet...

The moonlight glinted on the strap of the tote bag she'd carried into the bedroom with her. She hadn't dared leave the envelope containing the money anywhere that her daughter might find it. Or her mother either, she conceded uneasily, not totally convinced Mrs Ross would approve. Where had the money come from? Was it legal? Why, exactly, did Henry Sawyer want her to trace his wife?

CHAPTER TWO

A BAR of sunlight squeezed between the drawn blinds, causing the man lying in its path to raise one arm to protect his closed eyes. Despite the fact that it was early November, the weakening sun could still be annoyingly brilliant, penetrating even his eyelids and arousing him from sleep.

'Damn,' he muttered, rolling onto his side to escape its rays, and then stifling an oath when his outflung arm connected with a warm body that wasn't his. He slitted his lids. Dammit, he thought in frustration, he was in Lacey's bed. God knew what time it was. He didn't remember much since last night.

'You're insatiable, do you know that?'

Lacey's drowsy voice warned him that his careless movements had been misconstrued, and he abruptly withdrew his hand from her rounded hip. It was always the same: he invariably despised himself after going on one of his binges, and it was just hard luck that Lacey had born the brunt.

Despite the fact that his head was pounding, he rolled purposefully off the bed. He staggered a little as he got to his feet, but the room soon stopped spinning. Apart from a burning desire to use the bathroom, he considered he was in comparatively good shape.

'Don't go.'

Lacey's plea fell on deaf ears, however, as he emerged from the adjoining bathroom and looked for his clothes. 'Go back to sleep,' he advised her, wondering if he'd been wearing underwear when he'd left Jamaica Hill the night before. Well, to hell with it, he thought impatiently, and stepped into the tight-fitting jeans he found lying on the floor.

'I don't want to go back to sleep,' protested Lacey

20

Sheridan sulkily, turning to face him, giving him the full benefit of her voluptuous breasts. 'Alex, what are you rushing off for?' She teased a nipple. 'Come back to bed. It's barely ten o'clock.'

Alex reached for his shirt, the soft folds of beige-coloured chambray falling smoothly about his olive-skinned shoulders. He caught sight of his reflection in the mirrors of the dressing table opposite and scowled at the dissipation in his face. For God's sake, what was he doing to himself? What did he hope to achieve? By behaving irresponsibly, he was just playing into Conrad Wyatt's hands.

'I'm talking to you, Alex.' Lacey's tone had sharpened, and there was resentment as well as entreaty in her gaze. 'I thought you wanted to talk about Sheridan's Fancy. You're not the only stud in King's Montford. We were going to discuss him doing some screwing, as well.'

Alex winced at the vulgarity. Despite all the money she'd inherited when her husband died, Lacey was still a Philistine at heart. She'd had elocution lessons, and Edward himself had tried to instil some refinement into her. But Lacey would never be a lady. She enjoyed shocking people too much for that.

Still, he reflected bitterly, who was he to judge? He went to bed with her, didn't he? He wasn't too proud to accept her hospitality—and her booze. It was because of the generous quantities of expensive burgundy she'd poured down his throat the night before that he was feeling so awful now. If his head was throbbing, it wasn't her fault. He was a hypocrite even to contemplate that it was.

'I've got to go,' he said doggedly, pushing the tail of his shirt into his jeans and glancing round for his boots. Dammit, he knew he'd been wearing socks when he came here. Where were they? God, he hated the pounding in his head when he bent to look.

'You're not listening to me, Alex.' Lacey switched to a plaintive tone now. 'You know I hate it when you blank me. Why can't you stay and have a shower, and then we'll—?'

'No,' said Alex flatly, finding his socks at last and hopping about to put them on. He shoved his feet into his boots. 'I've got to speak to Guthrie. Some woman is coming for an interview this morning.'

'What woman?'

Once again, Lacey's expression had altered, and as if realising she was not going to change his mind with her nude body she thrust her legs out of bed and reached for her satin wrap. Watching her, Alex had to admit she was a good-looking woman. At her age, a lot of other females had turned to fat.

'I said, what woman?' she said now, catching his arm before he could put on his jacket, giving him a wounded look. 'Alex, why are you being so mean to me? You were so eager—so passionate—last night.'

Alex stifled a groan. Last night, he'd come here with the best of intentions. Lacey's stallion, Sheridan's Fancy, was exactly what he needed to boost the quality of his own horse-flesh, and he'd been prepared to do just about anything to meet her price. But this morning he was viewing the situation differently, his previous friendship with Edward Sheridan tarnished by this tawdry affair. Lacey was almost old enough to be his mother, for God's sake. And apart from that, did he really want to get involved with anyone else?

The air in the bedroom was suffocating suddenly, a combination of Lacey's heady perfume, sweat, and sex. He wanted to escape; he wanted to get on a horse—any horse—and ride until he'd outstripped his depression. But he knew it wasn't that simple; that it would take more than a simple horse ride to lift his mood. Until he got Rachel back, he didn't stand a chance of living a normal life.

Pulling free, he shrugged into his jacket. 'It's no one you know,' he told her briefly. 'Just someone who wants a job.' He checked his pockets for his wallet. 'I've got to go, Lace. I'll give you a call this afternoon.'

'You'd better.'

Lacey sounded aggressive, but Alex knew better. Despite

her sometimes coarse exterior, she could be hurt, just like anyone else. Which was probably why he hadn't severed their relationship, he conceded ruefully. Even if, just lately, he'd sensed that he was getting in too deep.

'I will. I promise,' he assured her now, eager to say anything to avoid a scene. He skimmed her lips with his, just to show there were no hard feelings, and then, raking impatient fingers through his tumbled hair, he left the room.

His Range Rover was where he'd left it, parked on the gravelled forecourt in front of the house. The air was delightful, fresh and dry, the sun burning off any lingering traces of frost from the night before. Considering it was November, the days were still surprisingly bright. If only his mood matched them, he thought grimly. Would he ever drag himself out of this hole?

The distance between Lacey's house and his own could be measured in minutes. The two estates ran side by side, with Jamaica Hill sweeping down into the valley. The River Way lay at the foot of Alex's property, widening into a lake among a copse of trees. The trees were bare now, but the sun shining on the water was brilliant, shadowing the willows that dipped down onto its banks.

There was a strange car parked near the entrance to the stables and Alex guessed it was the woman Guthrie had invited for an interview. Since all the stables' accounts had been computerised, his manager had employed a series of young women to do the job he'd previously done himself. The old man maintained he was too set in his ways to learn how to use a keyboard, but because his manner was brusque none of them had stayed very long.

Alex wasn't really in the mood to sit in on another interview, but he'd promised Guthrie to show his face and he was already fifteen minutes late. He scraped a hand across the night's stubble on his jaw and grimaced impatiently. He should have taken Lacey up on her offer of a shower. If he hadn't been so hung-over...

He pushed open the door of the Range Rover, ready to get

out, and then paused when the door to Guthrie's office opened and two people came out. One of them was his manager, unmistakable in his deerstalker and tweeds. But the other person was female. Was the interview over, or what?

He hesitated, torn by the desire not to get involved and an unwilling curiosity about the interviewee. It had certainly been brief, he reflected. Either that or she'd turned him down.

From what he could see, she was younger than the previous incumbent, with an unruly mass of permed blonde hair. Though not a teenager, he decided shrewdly. In black leggings and a tweed jacket, she looked nearer thirty than twenty.

But she was attractive, he conceded grudgingly. He couldn't see what colour eyes she had, but they were wideset and fringed with lashes darker than her hair. Her mouth was generous, too, and when she spoke Alex was surprised to see Guthrie's face crease with laughter. So what? he wondered, eyes narrowing. Was she a contender, after all?

Deciding he couldn't sit there like some sleazy voyeur any longer, Alex pocketed his keys and thrust his legs out of the car. He might as well show his face, he thought, and get it over with. It wasn't as if he cared what she thought of him.

The slamming of the Range Rover's door attracted their attention, as he'd known it would. But if he'd expected Guthrie to look relieved at his appearance he was disappointed. The woman looked towards the sound, too, and he wondered later if he'd only imagined the sudden apprehension in her expression. But it was quickly hidden, and when Guthrie brought her over to be introduced she smiled with just the right amount of deference.

'This is Kate Hughes,' the older man said gruffly, and Alex wondered if he was anxious that his employer shouldn't interfere. 'This is the boss, Kate. Mr Kellerman.' Then, to Alex again, he said, 'I was just going to show her round the yard.'

Alex nodded, his headache briefly forgotten as he parted the sides of his jacket to hook his thumbs into the front pockets of his jeans. 'I gather the interview was successful.' He couldn't remember Guthrie behaving so enthusiastically before. 'Are you interested in horses, Miss Hughes?'

'Not particularly.' At least she was honest. 'I haven't had the opportunity to deal with them before.' She smiled at Guthrie. 'But I'm interested in the job. And I'm computer-literate. I'm looking forward to working here; to learning all there is to know.'

'A daunting prospect,' remarked Alex dryly, wondering why her words seemed to strike such a disturbing chord inside him. It wasn't just that he was attracted by her appearance, although there was no denying that she was infinitely more attractive close to. He could now see that she had grey eyes, an unusual combination with her streaked blonde hair. Though that might not be natural, he reflected. Some women coloured their hair as frequently as they changed their lipstick these days. 'Where are you working at present?'

'I'm not—' she began, only to be baulked in whatever she was going to say by Guthrie's impatient exclamation.

'I have asked Kate all these questions!' he exclaimed shortly. He gave his employer a speaking look. 'I believe there are some messages for you up at the house.'

Alex conceded defeat. Whatever his opinion of Miss Hughes might be—and he wasn't entirely sure why he should have any misgivings in the first place—Guthrie was clearly delighted by his find. And he was the one who was going to have to work with her, and if she didn't do her job to his satisfaction he was the one who'd have to fire her, too. Alex, himself, couldn't object if she satisfied his manager. When he'd hired an assistant for him, he'd let his sympathies rule his head.

'Right,' he said now, using one hand to rake his aching scalp. 'I'll leave it up to you, Sam. I'm sure you know what you're doing.'

Guthrie took the implied reproof without comment, and Alex turned back to the Range Rover to drive up to the house. 'It was nice meeting you, Miss Hughes,' he said, over his shoulder. 'I'll see you later, Sam. Good luck.'

But, as he drove away, Alex wondered why he'd made such an issue of Sam Guthrie's decision. What was there about the Hughes woman that caused him such a feeling of unease? Was it her slight resemblance to Alicia Sawyer that had thrown him? Why did he have the feeling that employing Kate Hughes might create problems he hadn't even thought of yet?

Was it because of the way she'd looked at him? He didn't kid himself that she'd been attracted to him, but there was no denying there'd been a guarded interest in her gaze. He rubbed his jaw again, feeling the harsh bristles with some disparagement. He was flattering himself if he thought there'd been anything more than curiosity in her face.

Perhaps she knew his history. He scowled. Dammit, of course she knew his history. It wasn't as if you could live in King's Montford without hearing the rumours about Pamela's death. And his own behaviour afterwards had only reinforced the speculation. Why in God's name had he let the Wyatts take Rachel away?

But he couldn't think about them. Not in his present mood. The attractions of the bottle were still far too easy to justify, and turning to drink hadn't helped him before. On the contrary, it was because he'd been so devastated by what had happened to Pamela that he'd buried his grief in a bottle in the first place, allowing Conrad Wyatt to destroy what was left of his reputation.

It was a week before he saw Kate Hughes again.

He knew Guthrie had taken her on. The old Scotsman, who had worked for the Kellermans for the past thirty years, had made a point of telling him he had. 'She's an intelligent lassie,' he'd persisted, recognising Alex's scepticism. 'It'll be nice to have a female about the place again.'

Alex wasn't so sure. Apart from his long-standing association with Lacey Sheridan, he had had little time for women in recent years. Since Pamela's death, it had been a struggle to even hang onto the stables, and there was no doubt that opinion was still mixed about whether he'd had a hand in her death or not.

Which was why it was proving so hard to get his daughter back.

When Pamela was killed, he hadn't been able to think straight. He hadn't even known she was pregnant, for God's sake, and that news had left him reeling for weeks. He knew they'd been having problems, and the eventuality of them getting a divorce had crossed his mind. But Rachel had still been a baby. He'd been prepared to put up with a lot for her sake, but he hadn't realised that Pamela was having an affair.

When she died, all he'd really known for certain was that the baby she'd been carrying wasn't his. It had been months since he and Pamela had slept together; months since they had shared a bed. Not that that fact had helped his case; it had only reinforced the opinion that he'd had something to gain by her death. And the fact that her father had invested in the business, and would obviously pull his support if Pamela left him, had seemed to prove the point.

Still, that was behind him now, and despite his own reservations Alex had assured Guthrie that he had no objections to his decision to employ Kate Hughes. 'What was she doing before she applied for this position?' he'd asked idly, not sure why he really wanted to know.

'She worked for her father; but he died several months ago, and since then she's been looking for a job.'

'Ah.'

Alex had absorbed that information, aware of Guthrie's disapproval, and had decided not to ask the old man what her father's business was. He could always find out later—providing she stayed the course, he'd reminded himself dryly; but he doubted his manager would appreciate the pun.

Nevertheless, he felt an unwelcome charge of emotion a few days later, when he turned the corner into the stable yard and found their new employee forking hay into an empty stall. This was not what she was being paid for, and he objected to the familiarity. He had some valuable horseflesh boarded at the stables and he wondered if he'd been right to be suspicious about her. Had she taken the job to enable her to snoop around?

He frowned. Not that she was alone. The stable-yard was busy, with one of the young apprentices walking two of the mares to cool them down after the morning's gallop. He could see Guthrie himself at the far end of the yard where the stable block angled into the barns and storerooms. He was talking to one of the owners, who had an appointment to see Alex at eleven o'clock.

She must have heard his boot-heels striking the concrete apron that ran along the side of the building nearest to her, because she straightened as he appeared, stretching her back. He didn't know if she was aware of it—though his instincts told him she probably was—but as she flexed her spine her breasts were clearly outlined beneath the fine angora of her sweater.

Her long legs were once again encased in black leggings, which hugged their shape with provocative intent. He could even see the slight cleft that shaped her bottom, and he was annoyed to feel an unfamiliar pressure in his trousers.

His frown deepened. It had been a pretty lousy week for him, one way and another. He'd heard from his solicitor that the latest hearing into his bid to regain custody of his four-year-old daughter had been put back yet again, due to the Wyatts' delaying tactics, and he dreaded to think what they were telling her. But the longer they could maintain guardianship of the child, the better chance they had of sustaining their position. They'd already started arguing that Rachel hardly knew him and that, in any case, his household was no fit place for a little girl.

To add to his frustration, Lacey appeared to have taken umbrage because he'd had to refuse her latest invitation. In other circumstances, a couple of days at the races would have appealed to him, but he'd been afraid it might give her the wrong idea. He liked Lacey; he was fond of her; she was fun to be with. But their primary connection—so far as he was concerned, at any rate—was horses. He despised himself for allowing sex to get in the way of what had been a good friendship up till now.

In consequence, he was in no mood to be tactful with Kate Hughes. 'Exactly what do you think you're doing?' he demanded. 'I don't pay you to swill out the stalls. Or is this some kind of unpaid overtime?' He glanced at his watch. 'What is this? Your coffee break, or what?'

'I finished what I was doing, Mr Guthrie was with a client, and I could see Billy needed some help,' she retorted, with none of the deference he'd expected. Her voice was husky from her efforts and as she spoke the warm draught of her breath caressed his cheek. She seemed indifferent to his disapproval as she swept damp strands of hair behind her ears. 'Do you have a problem with that?'

Alex's mouth tightened. 'Obviously I do,' he told her shortly. 'And I'm not your father, Miss Hughes. If this is the way you used to speak to him, then perhaps you should remember where you are now.'

She coloured then, the skin of her neck and cheeks deepening to a fiery shade of pink. The change was appealing, giving her a vulnerability he hadn't expected, and his earlier reaction to her ignited in his gut.

'I'm sorry,' she said stiffly, and conversely he wanted to apologise for embarrassing her. It was disconcerting how easily she could arouse unwelcome feelings, and he found himself shaking his head.

'No, I'm sorry,' he muttered ruefully, thrusting his hands into his jacket pockets, almost as if he didn't trust himself not to reinforce his words with deeds. He grimaced. 'You'll have to forgive me. I don't usually take my grief out on the staff.'

'Your grief?' she echoed at once, and he realised how his statement could be misconstrued.

'Not literally,' he said dryly, his lips twitching at the prospect. 'No, I guess what I really mean is that I'm not in the best of moods.'

She moistened her lips with the tip of a pink tongue, her expression one of mild interest, and he guessed she expected him to explain. 'A personal matter,' he added briskly, surprised at the urge he had to confide in her. For God's sake, wasn't he in enough emotional turmoil as it was?

'They're the worst,' she said now, propping her chin on the handle of the pitchfork and looking up at him with sympathetic eyes. 'So you're not going to fire me today?'

'I'll give it more thought,' Alex promised lightly, finding himself fascinated by the impish smile that curled her lips. 'Does that mean you want to stay?'

'Why not?' Was she openly flirting with him now? He wondered if that was how she had disarmed Guthrie, who was usually known for his irascibility, not his charm. 'I just hope you'll have solved your problems by the time we meet again.'

'Unlikely,' remarked Alex wryly. Then, because he was becoming far too familiar with an employee, he brought their exchange to an abrupt halt. 'Excuse me,' he added, raising a hand in a gesture of farewell, and without waiting for her response he strode away across the yard.

But he was almost certain that she watched him go, the awareness of her eyes on his back causing an almost physical impact inside him. Irritation gripped him. He was behaving like an idiot even thinking about her, and the knowledge that he was becoming curious about her personal life really bugged him. Didn't he have enough to deal with as it was?

Nevertheless, her image remained in his thoughts for the remainder of the day and it was only sheer will-power that stopped him from asking Sam Guthrie what her background was. He could have checked the files. Whatever he lacked in a technical capacity, Guthrie was nothing if not thorough, and all her details would be neatly logged away in her personal folder.

But he didn't. Whether she'd been married, whether she was attached—she didn't wear a ring, but that meant nothing these days—whether she was in the habit of forming casual relationships was nothing to do with him. He had no intention of getting involved with anyone, least of all a woman he employed.

CHAPTER THREE

KATE watched Alex Kellerman walk away with a shiver of anticipation running down her spine. Despite the sudden way he had ended their conversation, she was sure she had made some progress in her quest to gain his confidence. He hadn't actually said anything; it was what he hadn't said that spoke volumes about his mood. She shivered again at the realisation that he had accepted her at face value. He had no idea that she was anything more than another employee.

Once again, using her own name had come in handy. Her National Insurance details were all in her married name. Of course, she hadn't corrected his assumption that she had never been married, but that was hardly an indictable offence.

She swallowed, turning back to forking hay with hands that weren't entirely steady. Talking to him had been more exhausting than she'd thought. Exhausting—and exhilarating, she admitted unwillingly. Whatever else he was, Alex Kellerman was definitely a most disturbing man.

Was that what Alicia Sawyer had thought?

Kate dug the fork into the bale of hay with more aggression than effect. She should know better than to start fantasising about Alex Kellerman, she told herself severely. If what she had heard was true, he was definitely not a man to be trusted.

Yet, in all honesty, she still knew precious little about him. Which was the main reason she had decided to apply for this job. Since his wife's death, there had been plenty of gossip, but nothing of substance. He seemed to have surrounded himself with people who weren't willing to talk.

Not to a stranger anyway, she amended, rubbing the back of her hand over her damp forehead. Despite his apparently doubtful reputation, he evidently inspired a sense of loyalty in his staff. She hadn't heard anyone say a hard word against him, even though it was obvious that the stables were having a struggle to survive.

The only thing she had learned was that he was trying to regain custody of his daughter. Apparently, her grandparents—her mother's parents, that was—had taken her away from Jamaica Hill just after their daughter had been killed. Which was reasonable enough, considering what Kate had read about Rachel's narrowly avoiding witnessing her mother's accident, but now they were refusing to give her up.

And, naturally, Alex wanted her back. She was his daughter, after all, and whatever kind of relationship he'd had with his wife Rachel was all he had left. Kate couldn't understand why he hadn't been granted custody before now, unless the Wyatts knew something about their son-in-law that they were using to keep the child themselves.

She frowned, picking up the fork again with renewed vigour. She wasn't here to speculate on Kellerman's relationship with his in-laws. She was here to find out what had happened to Alicia Sawyer, and so far she wasn't making a very satisfactory job of it.

Henry Sawyer wouldn't be pleased to think she was entertaining any sympathy for Alex Kellerman, she mused. When he'd turned up at her office a few days after giving her the assignment and learned what little progress she'd made in those few days, he'd been well peeved. She didn't know exactly what he'd expected, but as far as she was concerned she'd done everything she could.

Of course, he wasn't interested in hearing that she'd confirmed what he'd told her: that her contact in the local social security office had endorsed the fact that Alicia had worked for Alex Kellerman, and that as far as the authorities were aware she hadn't taken up any other employment since she left. Sawyer had already told her that the small account Alicia had had with the West Avon bank hadn't been drawn on for the past two months, and there were no credit card statements available either.

Kate had gone further, of course. She'd managed to find out that Alicia had no relatives in King's Montford, and that she hadn't been admitted to any hospital in the area under her own name. She'd shown her photograph in job centres and travel agents, she'd even shown it at the bus and train stations, but without any satisfactory result. It seemed that Alicia Sawyer had disappeared, just as her husband had said.

'So what do you intend to do next?' he'd demanded. And when Kate had looked a little doubtful he'd produced the advertisement which she was sure was why he'd come in. 'That's Alicia's job,' he'd declared, tossing the scrap of newsprint onto the desk in front of her. 'Why don't you apply for that?'

Her initial response had been one of incredulity. At no time in her father's long career had he ever gone undercover to get information, and the idea of passing herself off as a secretary had seemed completely over the top.

'Then I want my money back,' Sawyer had snapped angrily, and she could see he meant it. Which would mean telling Joanne that the skiing trip was off.

She'd despised herself afterwards, of course. Giving in to a man like Sawyer was not what being a private detective was all about. But there was no doubt that applying for the job was the best way of finding out what had happened to Alicia. So far, she'd had no luck in talking to anyone from the stables, and she'd consoled herself with the thought that her father might have had to amend his methods of detection in this case.

Which was how she came to be standing in the yard at Jamaica Hill helping Billy Roach with his chores. It was true she had finished the work that Mr Guthrie had given her, and she supposed she could have spent her free time reorganising the files. But Billy seemed her best bet as far as getting any information about Alicia Sawyer was concerned, and winning his gratitude, and his confidence, would go a long way towards proving she could be trusted.

All the same, it was hard work, and her back was aching. If Kellerman hadn't still been standing in the yard, talking to Guthrie and his companion, she'd have packed it in and gone back to the office. It was cold, and although she was sweating as she worked any break in her activities caused her to shiver. Or was it the awareness of danger? Was Kellerman really as innocent as he'd have everyone believe?

He was coming towards her again now, accompanied by the man who had been talking to Mr Guthrie, and she had to force herself to meet his narrow-eyed gaze. He was talking to his companion, but he was looking at her, and she made herself offer a small smile in response.

But after he was gone reaction set in and she shuddered. God, was she really trying to make him believe she was the kind of woman who took pleasure in flirting with men? Until she'd come to the interview here, she hadn't even owned a pair of leggings, let alone worn them. When she'd first put them on, her initial thought had been to hide her backside.

She shook her head. She had to stop thinking so negatively. Whether it was an act or not, she had succeeded in drawing Kellerman's attention to herself. If he thought she was ripe for an affair, however, she would have to disabuse him. Gaining his confidence was one thing; prostituting herself to satisfy Sawyer was something else.

Nevertheless, as she drove home that evening, she was unwillingly aware that she wasn't entirely indifferent to Alex Kellerman's attraction, and talking to him hadn't been as difficult as she'd expected either. On the contrary, for the first time since Sean's death, she'd met a man she felt at ease with. What a pity he was going to hate her when he found out why she was there.

The following morning she got the chance she'd been waiting for. Guthrie was away for the morning, and he'd left her in nominal charge of the office, so that when Billy Roach came to tell the manager he'd finished cleaning the tack Kate suggested he should take a break and join her for coffee.

'I've had my break, Miss Hughes,' replied Billy, with a rueful grimace. At sixteen, and a little over five feet in height, he was the youngest apprentice in the yard. He was also the least intelligent, according to the manager. 'If Mr Guthrie's not here, I should be getting back.'

'Oh, must you?' Kate adopted her most winsome expression. 'So I've got to have my coffee on my own.' She allowed her tongue to circle her lips in what she hoped was a provocative gesture. 'I thought you might like to sit and chat with me for a while.'

'Well, I would.' Billy shifted a little uncomfortably. 'But I do have work to do. And if Mr Guthrie came back and found me here—'

'He won't.' Kate stepped past him to close the door, and then turned to smile at him encouragingly. 'He's gone to Bristol, as you know. I don't suppose he'll be back until later this afternoon.'

Billy still looked doubtful. 'I don't think the other men would like it,' he murmured uneasily.

'Well, while you're thinking about it, I'll pour us both a cup of coffee,' declared Kate, moving towards the filter. She cast him a smile over her shoulder. 'Relax. If anyone comes, I'll tell them it was my idea.'

'As if they'd believe that.'

Billy was still uncertain, and Kate realised she'd have to work very hard to allay his fears. 'If it's any consolation, I don't think Mr Kellerman would object if he found out. He seemed very impressed with your work when I spoke to him yesterday.'

'He did?'

Billy was staring at her with eager eyes now and Kate felt terribly guilty for leading him on. 'Oh, yes,' she said, concentrating on adding milk to the coffee to avoid looking at him. 'When I said I was helping you, he implied you were one of the best apprentices he'd ever had.'

'Really?' Billy took the mug she handed him now and perched on a corner of her desk. 'How about that?' He chuckled, his earlier doubts forgotten for the moment 'And I thought both he and Mr Guthrie thought I was thick!'

Kate shook her head, half wishing she hadn't been so effusive, but Billy didn't want to let it go. 'Perhaps I should ask for a rise,' he mused, arching an inquisitive brow. 'This job doesn't pay much, you know. If I wasn't still living at home, I wouldn't be able to pay the rent.'

'Oh…' Kate drew a hasty breath. 'Well, I'm not sure this is the best time to ask Mr Kellerman for a rise,' she declared, horrified that he might quote her on this. She glimpsed the truculence in his eyes, and hurried on, 'You know things are pretty tight at the moment. If I were you I'd wait until next year.'

'Things are always tight,' muttered Billy glumly, burying his nose in the beaker of coffee, but Kate was relieved to hear the resignation in his voice. That was one thing about Billy: he was easily persuaded, but she determined not to get herself into that kind of corner again.

'I—I suppose it's been hard for Mr Kellerman,' she ventured instead, deciding she couldn't afford to waste this chance, however reckless it might be. 'Since his wife was killed, I mean,' she added tentatively. 'It can't have been easy, picking up the pieces of his life.'

Billy regarded her across the rim of his cup. 'You like Mr Kellerman, don't you?' he said, getting exactly the wrong message. He lowered his cup and grinned at her. 'All the ladies like Mr Kellerman, you know? Or they used to.'

Kate sighed. 'I do not—that is, I was being objective. I meant—well, according to Mr Guthrie, there have been—problems at the yard.'

In fact, Sam Guthrie had told her nothing of his employer's problems, and she could only hope that Billy didn't know that, or betray her confidence to the manager. She grimaced. She didn't think it was likely. The old Scotsman treated Billy as a pair of hands and nothing more.

'Problems?' Billy looked blank for a moment, and Kate wondered if she was wasting her time talking to him. But then, drawing his brows together, Billy gave her a thoughtful look. 'I suppose you mean when Allie walked out?'

Kate's jaw dropped. She felt like a player on a slot machine who had suddenly hit the jackpot. 'Allie' had to be Alicia Sawyer. God, and she'd doubted she had the time to get to the other woman's disappearance today.

But then, she'd imagined she'd have to wait while Billy told her about Pamela Kellerman's accident, and although that intrigued her it wasn't why she was here. But she'd been prepared to put up with that, so long as Billy eventually reached the point of Alicia's employment, although she had to admit she'd had doubts about how long it was going to take.

Yet now, quite incredibly, Billy had brought up the very thing she wanted, and she realised, belatedly, that he'd not been working at the stables when Pamela was killed. Kate could hardly contain her excitement at this development, and she struggled to find something to say that wouldn't arouse his suspicions.

'Allie?' she echoed at last, and then had to wait impatiently while he took another mouthful of his coffee before going on.

'Mrs Sawyer,' he agreed, wiping his mouth with the back of his hand. 'The woman who worked here before you. She liked me to call her Allie. She said it reminded her of when she was a little girl.'

Kate strove for a casual tone. 'But you say she—she walked out?' She waited a beat. 'D'you mean she was fired?'

'No.' Billy was indignant now. 'Mr Guthrie wouldn't have done that. He liked her.'

'Did he?' Kate wasn't sure how to go on. 'What do you mean, then?' She remembered just in time that she wasn't supposed to know anything about her. 'Um—didn't she turn up for work one morning, or what?'

'She just left,' said Billy glumly. 'She didn't even say goodbye. Mr Kellerman said—'

He broke off abruptly. A look of undisguised horror had darkened his face, and all the hairs on the back of Kate's neck rose up in sympathy. She was sure he'd remembered something significant, something that still had the power to fill him with terror. She leaned towards him, silently urging him to finish what he was saying, and then heard the sound that had panicked him into silence in the first place.

Footsteps were approaching, and Billy slammed his mug down onto the desk, spilling half its contents in the process. 'It's Mr Kellerman,' he muttered, catching sight of his employer through the window into the yard. 'Crikey, what am I going to do now?'

Kate, who had her own reasons for not wanting to encounter Alex Kellerman at that moment, gave an impatient shake of her head. 'You're only drinking a cup of coffee!' she exclaimed, hiding her impatience. 'If anyone's in trouble, it's me.'

Billy was not convinced and, wrenching open the door, he confronted his employer with a nervous grin. 'I—I was just leaving, Mr Kellerman,' he muttered. 'I cleaned out the tack room like Mr Guthrie said.'

Alex Kellerman frowned, but before he could make any comment Billy had scooted away across the yard. The older man looked after him, an expression of momentary speculation crossing his face. Then he turned to look at Kate as he entered the office, and she had to steel herself not to look as guilty as she felt.

'Is something wrong?' he asked, coming into the small office and closing the door. Like the stables themselves, and the other buildings that made up three sides of the rectangle, the office opened straight out into the yard. He leaned against the door, but that didn't stop the feeling Kate had that the room was suddenly smaller. His eyes alighted on the pool of coffee. 'Did I interrupt something?'

'Of course not.' Kate spoke a little sharply, but she

couldn't help feeling frustrated and it showed. 'I—Billy—
well, I asked him to join me for coffee. He—he was looking
for Mr Guthrie, that's all.'

'Really?'

'Yes, really.' Kate remembered she was supposed to be
trying to gain his confidence as well and forced a smile. 'I
suppose I shouldn't have done it, but it gets pretty lonely in
here when Mr Guthrie's away.'

'Does it?'

His responses were hardly encouraging, and because she
was far too aware of their isolation she took refuge behind
her desk. She would have to soak up the coffee Billy had
spilled, she reflected, but she'd do it later. She had no desire
to get any closer to Alex Kellerman than was absolutely necessary right now.

'I suppose it was too much to hope that you hadn't heard
the rumours,' he remarked after a moment, and this time Kate
had no chance to control the sudden heat that burned her
cheeks.

'I beg your pardon?' she said, her mind racing to find a
convincing explanation. Her knees felt weak. Had he heard
what she'd been asking Billy? Had he been outside the door
long before they'd heard the betraying clatter of his feet?

Kellerman straightened away from the door, and once
again Kate had to steel herself not to react. If she was going
to have any kind of success as a private investigator she had
to stop behaving like a scared rabbit. If he was angry with
her, so what? She hadn't done anything wrong.

Except...

Except take a job under false pretences. Except lie about
her reasons for being here. Not to mention the fact that she'd
accepted payment for investigating a woman's disappearance.
Oh, yes, she was sure he'd believe there was nothing wrong
about that.

He approached the desk and she stiffened. He was dressed
all in black and she wondered if that was why he seemed so
menacing today. Didn't he feel the cold? she wondered, her

eyes flickering over the opened collar of his black silk shirt. There was no trace of the goosebumps she was suffering in the strong-muscled column of his throat.

But it was his eyes that really disturbed her. They looked almost black in his hard, accusing face. She was forced to look at them, forced to look at *him*, forced to acknowledge his physical superiority. If he intended to fire her, there wasn't much she could do about it. He was not the sort of man to suffer any kind of interference in his private life.

'My wife's death,' he said now, the tips of his fingers just resting on the rim of her desk. A look of contempt crossed his face. 'That was what you were grilling Billy about, wasn't it? You wanted to know all the gory details about how she died.'

The breath expelled from Kate's lungs almost explosively. He didn't know, she realised weakly, hanging onto the edge of the desk herself for support. 'Um—no,' she stammered hastily. 'Your—your wife's accident is nothing to do with me. Besides, Billy wasn't here when it happened, was he? He's too young. I seem to remember it was about—well, several years ago.'

Kellerman's brows drew together. 'It was,' he agreed stiffly. 'Over two years ago, as you say.' His thin lips compressed. 'Not that that matters. Billy's been working here for almost a year. He's bound to have discussed it with the other men.'

'Well, he didn't discuss it with me.' Kate was relieved to hear that she sounded almost confident. 'That's not what we were talking about.' And then, before he could ask the obvious question, she added, 'Aren't you getting a little paranoid, Mr Kellerman? People do have other interests in their lives.'

'Do they?' But she could see the doubt in his expression. 'Sometimes, I feel as if they talk about nothing else.' He took a step back from the desk, and pushed his hands into the back pockets of his tight jeans, the spread sides of his leather jerkin exposing a taut midriff above his belt. 'You have every right to think I'm over-reacting, Miss Hughes. But I'm afraid I have become very sensitive in recent months.'

She could believe it, and, ridiculously, Kate knew a sudden desire to reassure him. This man, who only moments before had seemed to present a real threat to her existence, was actually inspiring her sympathy. It couldn't have been easy living with all the gossip, she conceded. And if he was innocent of any charge, as he professed, it must have been doubly hard.

If...

'It's—understandable,' she assured him, glancing behind her at the pot of coffee sitting warming on its stand. She hesitated for only a moment before coming to a decision. 'Er—can I offer you a drink, Mr Kellerman?'

He seemed certain to refuse, and she prepared herself for his rejection. But then, he seemed to change his mind. 'Why not?' he said, nodding towards the spillage Billy had created. A small smile touched his lips. 'I'll try not to make any more mess.'

Kate found herself returning his smile, and then hurriedly turned away to take a clean mug from the shelf. Was he teasing her? she wondered. Was he trying to make amends for his earlier harshness? She didn't know, but when he let down his guard he was really nice.

Nice!

She picked up the pot with rather less complacence. Dammit, *nice* was not an adjective she could use to describe him. Aggressive, perhaps; sarcastic, definitely; maybe even dangerous. And how did she know his affair with Mrs Sawyer hadn't started exactly like this?

Her breath caught in her throat, and her hand shook as she poured his coffee. Just for a moment, she'd wondered what it would be like to have an affair with him. With Alex Kellerman? She was appalled. That was scary. She felt exposed suddenly, as if a sensitive layer of skin had been removed.

She used both hands to offer the mug of coffee to him,

just in case her shaking hands warned him of how disturbed she was. 'D'you have any sugar?' he asked, as she was congratulating herself at succeeding, and she saw she hadn't offered him any milk either.

'Sorry,' she murmured, handing him the packet of sugar. There were no social niceties in the office 'Um—do you take milk too? I'm afraid I forgot to ask.'

'Black and sweet,' he assured her wryly, another of those small smiles playing about his mouth. 'Mmm, that's good,' he added, after tasting it. 'Slightly stewed, but full of flavour.'

Kate groaned. 'You don't like it!' she exclaimed. She gestured towards the filter. 'Would you like me to make a fresh pot?'

'No. This is fine.' He glanced behind him for a chair. 'May I sit down?'

'Of course.' Kate lifted her shoulders. 'It's your office.'

'So it is.' He grimaced and dropped down into an old leather chair that was situated beside the electric heater. 'Mmm.' He stretched out his long legs. 'That's better.' He crossed his booted ankles. 'Now, d'you want to tell me what Roach was doing here?'

She should have known he wouldn't forget, thought Kate, subsiding into her own chair with some reluctance. 'Roach?' she said thoughtfully, giving herself a few moments to compose an answer. 'Oh, you mean Billy,' she added needlessly. 'I can't remember now.'

'I believe he implied he'd been looking for Guthrie,' Alex prompted, his eyes sharp as they appraised her across the rim of his mug.

'Oh, yes, that's right. He was,' Kate said gratefully. 'That's why he came to the office.' She put her mug aside. 'Were you looking for Mr Guthrie, too?'

'As a matter of fact, I wanted to speak to you,' Alex remarked now, instantly banishing her smugness.

'To me?' she got out faintly. 'Why? Is something wrong?'

'What could be wrong?' he countered now, and she

thought again how reckless she'd been in coming here. When Alex set down his mug on the floor beside his chair and steepled his hands across his flat stomach, she swallowed convulsively. But all he said was, 'I thought it was time I got to know something about the newest member of my staff.'

Kate's mouth felt unpleasantly dry. 'But didn't Mr Guthrie—?'

'Oh, sure. Sam has no complaints about you. I'm sure you know you charmed him right from the start.'

'But not you.' The words were out before she could prevent them. 'I mean—well, I don't mean that exactly.' She inwardly cringed. 'Um—do you have a problem? About my work, I mean.'

'Why should I?' Alex leaned forward in his seat, resting his arms along his spread thighs. 'But your working here is bound to cause repercussions. I just wondered what your family thought about that.'

Kate expelled an uneven breath. 'My—family is quite happy about me working here,' she told him, refusing to think about what her mother had said when Kate had told her what she intended to do.

'So they don't think I'm as wicked as the press has painted me?' His eyes were intent. 'They don't believe I killed my wife for her money?'

Kate stared at him. 'For her money?' she echoed blankly, and he stifled a bitter oath.

'Oh, haven't you heard that part of the story?' he queried scornfully. 'Well, don't worry. If you stick around here long enough, you will.'

Kate drew a breath. 'It must have been very—painful for you.'

'The standard response.' His lips twisted. 'They all say that.' He paused. 'Well, those who believe me—or say they do, at any rate—assure me of their sympathy. I think I'm supposed to be grateful, or something like that.'

'And you're not?'

Once again, Kate spoke without considering what she was saying, and Alex's face mirrored a faint respect. 'Do you think I'd tell you?' he asked, and she caught her breath. His lips twisted. 'I don't have a satisfactory answer for what happened to Pamela. I'm sorry she's dead, but the pain came long before she fell off the horse.'

Kate didn't know what to say. This was not a conversation she had ever expected to be having with him. She'd never dreamt that Alex Kellerman might talk about his wife's death to her. And if there had been money involved, people did crazy things.

'But I didn't come here to talk about me,' he said, getting abruptly to his feet, and Kate realised that she was under his mental microscope once again. He came towards the desk, idly straightening the pile of letters and bills she had yet to deal with. 'You never did tell me what you did before you took this job.'

'I worked for my father,' said Kate at once, glad she could answer truthfully. But then, when that obviously wasn't enough, she added, 'He—he had a small—insurance agency in—in Bath.'

'Not in King's Montford?'

'No.'

'And you didn't think of continuing with the agency?'

Kate shook her head. 'No. It—it wasn't the same after my father died.'

He conceded the point, but he still seemed curious. Was it only her imagination, or was he as suspicious of her answers as she was of his? 'I still don't see why you'd want to do this job,' he said at last. His eyes narrowed. 'It isn't as if there's any responsibility involved.'

'I don't need responsibility.' Kate could have added that she'd had more responsibility than he could imagine in her comparatively short life. 'I obviously wanted a job, and there aren't that many to choose from. Not—not everyone wants to employ someone as—as old as me.'

He gave her an old-fashioned look. 'Am I suppose to answer that?' he asked levelly, and her skin burned at the irony in his face. The office wasn't large, and she was far too aware of his maleness. He could have no idea how inexperienced she was at fencing with any man.

'I—I just meant a lot of employers are looking for younger women,' she explained awkwardly. 'I'm sorry if you thought I was fishing for compliments. I—I'm not like that.'

'What are you like, I wonder?' he mused, and her throat tightened almost convulsively. 'Are you one of those females who imagine it would be a thrill to sleep with a killer?'

Kate gulped. 'You're not a killer!' She refused to consider the rest of what he'd said.

'How do you know?'

She didn't, of course, and a few moments ago she'd have believed almost anything of him. 'I just know,' she declared, somewhat naively. 'Do you think I'd have taken this job if I'd thought you'd—you'd—?'

'Murdered my wife?' Alex was laconic, and she reluctantly nodded.

'When my father was alive, he always used to say I was a good judge of character,' she agreed, getting to her feet.

'Your father?' He paused. 'The insurance agent.'

'That's right.' She was grateful he had reminded her. 'I'm sure if you'd met him you'd have liked him, too.'

'Was he as gullible as you?' he asked sardonically, and Kate took a steadying breath.

'I don't think I'm gullible, Mr Kellerman. Just because I'm prepared to give somebody the—the benefit of the doubt.'

'And you think your father would approve of you working for me? Someone of your—age and intelligence typing statistics into a computer? Come on, Miss Hughes, do you really expect me to believe that?'

Kate shrugged. 'Perhaps I'm not as intelligent as you think…?' she began, and then flinched when he leant towards her.

'And perhaps you're too damn clever for your own good.'

His lips thinned. 'I'm not stupid, Miss Hughes. I can recognise a phony when I see one, whatever your editor thinks!'

'My editor!' Kate could have collapsed with relief, but instead she forced herself to meet his shrewd gaze. 'I don't have an editor,' she denied swiftly. 'Whatever you think you know. I'm not a journalist, Mr Kellerman. I've never worked for a newspaper in my life.'

'Can you prove it?'

'Can I—?' Kate tried to think. 'I—journalists usually have press cards, don't they?' She fumbled to get her handbag out of the drawer beside her. 'You can look through my personal belongings, if you like.'

Too late, she remembered her investigator's licence tucked inside her wallet, but she needn't have worried. 'I don't imagine you'd carry such an incriminating thing around with you,' Kellerman said, dismissing her offer. His expression softened somewhat, nevertheless. 'Do you swear you're not working for any publication, tabloid or otherwise?'

'Yes.' There was conviction in her voice.

'No freelance assignments? No docu-dramas for television?'

'No.' But despite the relief her knees were trembling. 'Do you believe me? I've never worked for the media.'

He studied her flushed face for what seemed like for ever, and then gave what she hoped was a gesture of assent. 'Okay,' he said at last. 'Okay, I believe you. But if I find out you've been lying...'

He didn't bother to finish the threat, but Kate knew what he meant. There'd be no second chances if he found her out. 'I think you've made your feelings very plain, Mr Kellerman,' she declared stiffly, her nails digging into her palms.

She was grateful that he seemed to accept that as a dismissal, and when he moved towards the door she sank down into her chair again and expelled an exhausted breath. But that didn't stop her from wishing she could just hand in her notice and leave while she still had all her faculties. She was very much afraid that Alex Kellerman was far more dangerous than she'd ever imagined.

CHAPTER FOUR

ALEX shoved the weights to their fullest extent for the final time and then lay panting, trying to get his breath back. Hell, he was out of condition, he thought disgustedly. Okay, he'd been pushing himself hard for the last couple of hours, but lifting the bar that last time had almost finished him off. He'd been spending too many nights with a bottle instead of with a woman, he reflected wryly. If there was one thing to say for sex it was that it didn't make you fat.

He heaved a sigh and got up from the bench-press, flexing his shoulders as he did so. What he needed was a shower, that was all, he assured himself. He'd feel a damn sight better when he got out of this sweaty gear. Then, when he was sure he'd eliminated all his frustration, he'd go and pick up Rachel. These additional visits were one concession his recent visit to court had granted him, and he had no intention of doing anything to blow the privilege now.

Even if the thought of going to the Wyatts' house to collect her still bugged him. He'd have much preferred it if his solicitor could have arranged for him to meet his daughter at a neutral point. But it was probably better for Rachel not to have to deal with too many strangers, he conceded. The muscles in his stomach tightened at the thought of losing her for good.

As he left the gym, which was in the basement of the house, and mounted the stairs to the first floor, he found himself thinking of Kate Hughes. He was slightly ashamed of the way he had treated her the previous day. He was well aware that he had intimidated the woman for no good reason. He had had no grounds for accusing her of being anything more—or less—than she claimed. Would she understand the pressure he was under if he told her about Rachel? She'd said she didn't believe he was a murderer, but that was before he'd practically accused her of working for the gutter press.

He reached his bedroom and crossed the floor to his bathroom, shedding his vest and shorts on the way. Then, kicking off his trainers, he stepped into the shower cubicle, running the water hot at first to sluice all the stickiness from his skin.

As he soaped his shoulders, he considered why he'd suddenly thought of Kate Hughes. Was it because of the way he'd behaved with her that had persuaded him to work out before going to Wyvern Hall? Perhaps he was afraid he'd let Conrad Wyatt arouse his anger. If he went there filled with resentment he'd be playing right into his father-in-law's hands.

Perhaps he should be grateful to the Hughes woman, he thought, returning to the bedroom. As he towelled his hair dry, he wondered what she thought of him now. He supposed he owed her an apology for coming on so strong, and he hoped he hadn't upset her. Guthrie wouldn't be very pleased if his protégée decided to take a hike.

He blew out a weary breath, looking round the room without pleasure. This was one of the smaller bedrooms. He'd moved out of the master suite when Pamela died. It needed some redecoration, but these days he had no enthusiasm for anything. If—when—he got Rachel back again, things would be different, he assured himself. He'd begin to feel that this was a real home again.

The Wyatts' estate was situated on the other side of King's Montford. Conrad Wyatt's family had farmed the land for over a hundred years, and although the old man himself no longer took an active part in running the estate he had a very efficient manager to do the job for him.

Alex had always known that Conrad regretted the fact that his wife had been unable to have any more children after Pamela was born, and when Pamela herself was expecting Rachel her father had hoped she would have a boy. At that time, though, it hadn't seemed important. Alex had assumed he and Pamela would eventually have a son. He hadn't known then that Pamela was going to be unfaithful, or that the second child she carried wouldn't be his.

It was impossible not to feel some emotion, Alex thought as he drove through the gates of Wyvern Hall. He might not have loved his wife when she died, but that didn't alter the fact that this was where she'd been born. Where he'd come to visit, when he and Pamela had first got to know one another; and where her father had voiced the suggestion that when he died they should move into the house.

He'd even asked Alex to consider changing his name to Wyatt. Alex's own father was dead, so he hadn't seen anything wrong in that. But Alex had. The Kellermans might not have such illustrious forebears, but under his direction the Kellerman stables were beginning to make an enviable name for themselves. There was no way Alex was going to deprive his heir of his real heritage, and his relationship with Conrad Wyatt had deteriorated from then on.

Even so, Alex had always tried to be civil to the man. He'd had no quarrel with Pamela's father, and he'd always hoped that some day they could really be friends. But then Pamela was killed, and Conrad had accused his son-in-law of contriving the 'accident.' Even Pamela's mother, who had remained neutral throughout most of their marriage, had been forced to take her husband's side.

There was little wonder, Alex reflected now, that he'd been shattered. His whole world had been falling apart, and the only solace he'd found was when he was too drunk to know what was going on. Rachel had been too young, too vulnerable, to offer him any comfort. Little wonder that her grandfather had found it so easy to convince the authorities that he and his wife should look after her until her father was capable of doing so.

Alex's hands tightened on the wheel at the unwelcome memory. But he knew it wouldn't do to go and meet Conrad Wyatt in a hostile frame of mind. He had to convince the

Wyatts he meant to regain custody of his daughter; that he was the fit and proper person to bring her up.

And he was, he told himself fiercely. Any bitterness he had left was all directed towards himself. He'd been a fool, but he'd learned his lesson the hard way. If he got Rachel back, he'd never act so stupidly again.

Julia Wyatt opened the door to him herself. Alex, who had been expecting to encounter the dour housekeeper, Mrs Gellis, felt an immediate sense of apprehension. Although Pamela's mother had always been less antagonistic than her husband, she was not in the habit of answering doors; not when she had a perfectly good member of staff to do it for her.

'Oh—Alex,' she said, almost as if she hadn't expected it to be him. She must have heard the car, he thought. Her sitting room was at the front of the house. 'I'm afraid I've got some bad news for you. Um—Rachel isn't very well.'

Alex pushed his hands into the pockets of his overcoat. It was a cold day and he had worn the long cashmere garment because he'd intended to take Rachel to the park. He'd planned that they would feed the ducks, and then go back to Jamaica Hill for lunch. In the afternoon, he'd been going to take her down to the stables. One of the mares had foaled and he was sure she'd love to see the spindly-legged colt.

But now...

'She's ill?' he asked, aware that his tone was brusque, but he couldn't help it. Of all the stunts he'd expected Conrad Wyatt to pull, he'd never anticipated anything like this.

'She's not ill exactly,' demurred Julia, glancing somewhat nervously over her shoulder. 'She's got a nasty little cold, and I don't think she should go out on a day like this.'

'*You* don't think?' asked Alex harshly. He was fairly sure this was all her husband's idea. But it was a damp, cold morning, and he took a breath to calm himself. Then, putting a booted foot on the step, he asked, 'May I see her?'

'Oh, I'm not sure—' began Julia, and then broke off abruptly when her husband's voice sounded behind her.

'Who is it, Julia?' he was demanding. 'It's far too cold to be standing at the door.' Then he saw Alex, and his expression hardened contemptuously. 'Oh, it's you.' He turned to his wife. 'Haven't you told him that Rachel can't go out today?'

'Well, yes—'

'She's told me, Conrad,' broke in Alex levelly, aware that his behaviour now was crucial. 'I was saying that I'd like to see her anyway.'

'You can't.' Conrad Wyatt didn't mince his words. 'She's—ah—she's sleeping. Isn't that right, Julia?' He exchanged a look with his wife, and Alex wondered what else was said in that silent stare. He turned back to his son-in-law, his eyes mirroring his triumph. 'I'm sorry to disappoint you, Kellerman, but there it is.'

Alex's hands curled into fists in his pockets. He would have liked nothing better than to stuff one of them down Conrad Wyatt's throat. The man was actually enjoying this, and no wonder. It would be another week before Alex could arrange to see Rachel again.

But Alex knew better than to argue with him. Conrad would like nothing better than to be able to tell a judge that he'd been threatened by his son-in-law. It would also add weight to what Conrad had always maintained about the accident: that Alex was violent and untrustworthy, and no fit guardian for the child.

'So am I,' Alex said now. 'Sorry, I mean.' He addressed himself to Julia. 'Will you let me know how she is tomorrow?'

'Oh—yes.' Julia glanced at her husband for his approval, before going on. 'But I'm afraid—'

'I know.' Alex was sardonic. 'I won't be able to visit her tomorrow. Just give her my love, will you? I'm sure I can trust you to do that.'

'Are you implying—?' began Conrad angrily, but Alex was already walking back to the Range Rover. Pretending he didn't hear, he opened the door and coiled his considerable length behind the wheel. Raising one hand in farewell, he started the powerful engine, deliberately churning up the gravel as he gunned the motor down the drive.

But once he was out on the King's Montford road again his spurt of defiance vanished. In spite of all his efforts, he was no further forward than before. And the knowledge that he wasn't going to spend the day with his daughter was like a burning pain inside him. At times like these, he wanted to cry like a baby for the way he'd screwed up his life.

But there was no point in letting Conrad Wyatt's attitude get to him, and he decided to drive to the Wayside and make his peace with Lacey instead. He had spoken to her in the last couple of days and she'd seemed more amenable. But that was on the phone. Who knew how she'd react if he turned up in person?

He decided to swing by Jamaica Hill first. He'd told his housekeeper he'd be in for lunch and she was making her special chocolate pudding just for Rachel. He knew Agnes Muir would be disappointed that the little girl wasn't joining them, just as he was. The elderly Scotswoman had supported him throughout all his dealings with the Wyatts.

He turned in at the gates and then had to brake hard to avoid a loitering teenager. The girl was hanging about inside the gates, apparently undecided as to whether to walk up to the house or turn off towards the stable block. She was fairly tall and slim, dressed in a short pleated skirt and a parka. He was sure he didn't know her, yet there was something strangely familiar about her startled face.

He rolled down his window. 'Can I help you?' he asked shortly. He wasn't really in the mood to talk to some strange schoolgirl, who was probably here to ask about a job. He and Guthrie got them all the time: girls who were horse-mad and wanted nothing more than to brush the animals' coats or muck out the stalls in their spare time. Most of them couldn't afford the cost of riding lessons, and working with the horses meant they sometimes got lucky and had the chance to hack around the paddock.

The girl looped her haversack over her shoulder and looked at him doubtfully. 'I—er—I was looking for my mum,' she said awkwardly. 'She—er—she works here. Her name's Kate. Kate—'

'Kate Hughes?' asked Alex, and the girl coloured guiltily.

'Yes. Kate Hughes,' she agreed hurriedly, and he guessed her mother had told her not to come here.

'You're her daughter?' Alex was surprised. Not because Kate wasn't a good-looking woman, but because he hadn't known she was married. If indeed she was. And it also explained that unfamiliar resemblance. He shook his head. 'If you get in the car, I'll take you down to the yard.'

'Oh, I don't—'

'I'm Alex Kellerman,' he informed her flatly. 'I'm sure your mother's warned you not to get into cars with strange men, but I happen to own this place.'

'I know.' Her eyes widened then, as if she was afraid she shouldn't have made such an admission. 'Well—' She hesitated. 'If you don't mind, that would be cool.'

Cool!

Alex grimaced and thrust open the door nearest to her. 'Get in,' he advised her tersely, and she swiftly swung her long legs over the seat. 'Shouldn't you be in school?' he asked as she slammed the door, and she gave him a rueful grimace.

'That's what Mum's going to say, I know, but I'm not going back.' She pursed her lips. 'Not today anyway.'

Alex frowned, not altogether unhappy at the diversion. 'Is something wrong?' he asked. 'Couldn't whatever it is have waited until tonight?'

'Mum's going to say that, too.' She gave him another doubtful look. 'She's really hot on getting a good education and all that.' She hunched her shoulders. 'But sometimes it's not as easy as she thinks.'

Alex put the car into gear. 'You're having problems,' he remarked dryly. 'Convincing people you're telling the truth can be pretty tough. I know.'

'I s'pose you do.' She glanced sideways at him. Then her

colour deepened again. 'I'm sorry. I shouldn't have said that. I don't really know anything about you.'

'That hasn't stopped plenty of other people from passing their opinion,' responded Alex, with some irony. And then he smiled. It was refreshing to meet someone who admitted to having preconceived ideas. 'So, as I'm such an authority, why don't you tell me what's troubling you?' He examined her face critically. 'I guess you go to the comprehensive in town.'

'Lady Montford,' she agreed, with a nod. 'I've been going there for over a year.'

'And you're finding the work too hard, is that it?' asked Alex gently, only to have her fix him with an indignant look.

'No!' she exclaimed. 'I don't find the work hard. Well, not especially. I'm not brilliant at maths, but I'm pretty good at everything else.' She sniffed. 'That's part of the trouble,' she muttered in an undertone, stiffening as she saw the roof of the stables through the trees.

Alex wished the journey had been longer. He had enjoyed talking to her, and he was loath to let her go without finding out what was wrong. 'So what's the problem—er—you didn't tell me your name?'

'Joanne.'

'—Okay, Joanne.' A thought occurred to him. 'You're not being bullied because they think you're a swot?'

'A what?'

She turned to gaze at him, and he realised they probably had other names for it these days. 'Because you're prepared to learn and they're not,' he explained, feeling very old suddenly.

'Oh, you mean a nerd.' She grimaced. 'No.'

Alex pulled a wry face, but they'd already reached the stable yard and he switched off the engine. 'Whatever it is, I'm sure if you discuss it with your mother she'll understand.'

'You think?' Joanne pulled a face. 'You don't know Mum like I do. She doesn't seem to understand how hard it is to stay friends with girls who think you're just a wimp.' She sighed. 'Have you ever done something you know was wrong and regretted it later, Mr Kellerman? Like, you want to put it behind you, but some people won't let you forget?'

Alex's brows drew together. What was this? he wondered. Some new way Conrad Wyatt had devised to disarm him and induce him to confess? He shook his head. No, that was crazy. This was Kate Hughes's daughter. He thought even Conrad would draw the line at using a child to do his dirty work.

'Look,' he said evenly, 'everyone does something they regret sometimes.' He grimaced. 'In my case, it was getting married to the wrong woman, but we won't go into that.' He paused. 'What can you have done that's so outrageous? You're—what? Thirteen? Fourteen?'

'I'm twelve.'

'There you are then. You're twelve—' he grinned at her haughty expression '—going on twenty. What can you have done to warrant that long face?'

'You don't have to be old to break the law,' Joanne retorted, gazing at him defensively. 'Oh, God, Mum's going to kill me when she finds out.'

Alex blinked. She was so serious. Whatever she'd done, she obviously believed it would cause her mother some grief. So, what? Missing lessons? Mouthing off at her teacher? *Taking drugs?* As she gathered her haversack to her chest, preparing to get out, he felt an unexpected twinge of alarm.

'You're not—' he began as she reached for the door handle, and then stopped himself before he could go on. This was crazy, he thought. He'd just met her. This girl meant absolutely nothing to him.

'I'm not what?' she asked, a small ladder in her tights delineating the bony curve of her knee. There was something fragile about that ladder; it made her look vulnerable. And, although he'd determined not to say any more, he couldn't help it.

'You're not—sniffing glue, or anything like that?' he

asked unwillingly, choosing the least likely option he could think of, and she gasped.

'No, I'm not,' she told him shortly. 'I'm not stupid, Mr Kellerman. And I don't do drugs either, even though I have been offered them.'

Alex was horrified. To hear that this child had already been offered drugs at her young age filled him with anger. Dear God, he thought, where was it all going to end? When were children allowed to be children, for pity's sake?

'I'm glad to hear it,' he said now, making an effort to hide his real feelings. 'And if it's not drugs I don't think you have anything to worry about.'

'That's all you know,' she muttered rudely, getting out of the Range Rover and hauling her bag out after her. 'You try telling Mum that I didn't want to go shoplifting last term.'

He suspected she hadn't meant to tell him, and judging from her expression she regretted it as soon as the words were out. But she didn't say anything in her own defence. She probably thought she'd be wasting her time, he reflected, watching her a little ruefully as she clumped off across the yard.

He was going to have to leave her to it. He prepared to do a three-point turn to go up to the house. But before he could accomplish this it became obvious that she didn't know which way to go, and, stifling the voice that was warning him not to get involved, he turned off the engine and swung out of the car.

'Hey!' His initial yell didn't attract her attention, and, slamming the car door, he tried again. 'Joanne!' He used her name this time. 'Where are you going? The office isn't along there. It's over here.'

She halted, turned, and came back to him with obvious reluctance, the sturdy Doc Martens she was wearing giving her long legs a stalk-like appearance. In that respect she resembled her mother, too, he conceded. One of the first things he'd noticed about Kate was her long legs.

But before she could reach him the door that led to her

mother's office flew open, and Kate herself emerged looking dismayed. 'Joanne!' she exclaimed, ignoring Alex for the moment in favour of her daughter. Then, acknowledging his presence with a nervous glance, she went on, 'What on earth are you doing here?'

'Mum—'

'Shouldn't you be in class?' Kate didn't wait for her to finish before examining her watch. 'It's only eleven o'clock.' Another quick glance in Alex's direction, and then she said, 'Nothing's wrong, is it? Your grandmother hasn't—'

'Nan's fine,' Joanne said flatly, trudging nearer.

'Then why is Mr Kellerman—?'

'I met her at the gate.' Against his better judgement, Alex sauntered up to them, noticing Kate was shivering in spite of her ankle-length skirt and woollen cardigan. 'Hadn't you better go inside, before you catch a chill?'

'What?' She looked up at him almost blankly for a moment and he realised she was more upset than he'd thought. 'Oh, yes.' Dark lashes shadowed her grey eyes as she directed her daughter towards the lights of the office behind her. 'I've just made some tea, Joanne. Go and pour us both a cup.'

Alex's lips twitched. 'That's very civil of you after yesterday.'

'Oh—' Once again, he saw a trace of anxiety in her face. 'I didn't mean—' He knew exactly what she'd meant, but he didn't make it easy for her. 'That is, if you'd like to join us, Mr Kellerman, then naturally—naturally you'd be very welcome.'

'Would I?'

He regarded her quizzically. It was so easy to disconcert her, he thought, and he knew an unexpected feeling of regret that she was married and therefore out of his reach. With the experiences he'd had, there was no way he'd put any other man through what he'd had to go through, but nevertheless he had to admit he was intrigued by his newest employee.

'Of course,' she said now, squaring her shoulders, and he realised she expected him to accept.

'Some other time,' he said, nodding towards the open doorway Joanne had just passed through. 'And go easy on your daughter, hmm? I think she's having a tough time at the moment.'

'You think what?' Kate stared at him coldly now and he guessed she resented his remark. 'I don't think the way I treat my daughter is anything to do with you, Mr Kellerman.' She straightened her spine, and then added with some vehemence, 'I don't think you're in any position to judge, do you?'

That stung, particularly this morning with the memory of Conrad Wyatt's latest tactics still sticking in his throat. 'Perhaps not,' he conceded coolly, choosing not to argue with her. 'I was merely offering an opinion. If I were her father—'

'But you're not,' she broke in heatedly. 'Joanne's father is dead, Mr Kellerman. He was killed in a car crash when she was barely two years old.'

'I'm sorry—'

Alex felt chastened, but this time Kate made a gesture of defeat. 'I'm not,' she told him flatly. 'And if that sounds hard to you, well—that's how I feel.' She took a breath. 'You see, he wasn't alone in the car when he died.'

'Ah...'

Alex nodded, and his understanding seemed to bring a change of heart. 'If I was rude just now,' she murmured, 'I'm sorry.' She glanced over his shoulder. 'Is your daughter waiting in the car?'

'My daughter's not coming,' he informed her firmly, not at all surprised that she should know where he'd been. The grapevine at the stables was quite efficient, and he hadn't hidden his delight at the prospect of seeing Rachel again from Mrs Muir, or Sam Guthrie, for that matter.

'Oh.' She actually looked sympathetic. 'There's nothing wrong, is there? Is she coming another day?'

'Not if my father-in-law has anything to do with it,' re-

marked Alex pleasantly. Then, because the temptation to confide in her was too inviting, he rocked back on his heels and
turned towards the car. 'I like your daughter,' he added, as
a parting observation. His lips twisted. 'You must have been
a teenager yourself when she was born.'

CHAPTER FIVE

'I'M NOT sure your father would approve of what you're doing, Kate.'

Ellen Ross confronted her daughter across the supper table that evening, primed, no doubt, by Joanne that her investigation at the stables wasn't as straightforward as she'd have had them believe.

'I don't know what you mean, Mum,' Kate protested now, giving Joanne an irritated look. 'And if someone hadn't been playing hookey we wouldn't be having this conversation.'

'No, that's probably true.' Ellen Ross turned her attention to her granddaughter now, as Kate had hoped she would. 'I can't believe you behaved so recklessly, Joanne. What were you thinking of?'

Joanne hunched her shoulders. 'I just got caught up in it,' she said defensively. 'I didn't know what they were planning to do until I got there.'

'"There" being Daltons department store,' put in Kate dryly. 'You realise you're going to have to tell Mr Coulthard what's been going on?'

'Oh, Mum!'

'Well, there's no other way to handle it,' declared Kate reasonably. 'If you own up, I doubt if Daltons will bring a charge.'

'Bring a charge!' Joanne was horrified. 'Mum, I only took a lipstick, nothing else.'

'It's still shoplifting, Joanne,' replied her mother firmly. 'You knew it was wrong. That's why you stayed away from school.'

'I stayed away from school because—because they expected me to go with them again.' Joanne grimaced. 'He won't expect me to grass on the others, will he?'

'*Grass!*' Her grandmother was appalled. 'Joanne, where do you get your expressions from?'

'Television,' said Kate flatly. 'And Mr Coulthard will ask you who was with you.' She bit her lip. 'I suppose whether you tell him or not is up to you.'

Joanne slumped over the table. 'Oh, God,' she groaned, 'I can't go back to that school again.'

'You don't have any choice,' said Kate, getting up to clear the dishes. 'Joanne, you're going to have to face those girls and tell them you're not a thief. You made a mistake, that's all. If they don't like it—well, it's not the end of the world. You'll make new friends who don't think you're a wimp because you don't get your kicks at other people's expense.'

'That's easy for you to say.'

'Actually, it's not easy for me to say,' replied her mother, running hot water into the sink. She cast Joanne a rueful look. 'As a matter of fact, it's very hard. I don't like the idea that you've got to deal with something like this in your second year at Lady Montford. But I'm sure you wouldn't like me to fight all your battles for you.'

'I suppose not.' Joanne straightened up reluctantly. 'But you will come with me to see Mr Coulthard tomorrow, won't you?'

'If I can get the time off,' agreed Kate, realising she'd have to ask Mr Guthrie. He might not be very pleased. As with Alex Kellerman, she'd never mentioned having a daughter to him.

'Will you have to ask Mr Kellerman?' asked her daughter at once, and Kate was reminded of her employer's remarks about Joanne. But before she could comment the girl turned to her grandmother. 'He's drop-dead gorgeous, Nan. Have you seen him?'

Ellen Ross's lips turned down. 'I've seen his picture in the newspaper,' she said dismissively. 'And "gorgeous" isn't an expression I'd have used.'

'Well—sort of brooding, then,' amended Joanne. 'And sexy. I bet Mum's noticed that, if nothing else.'

'Joanne!'

'That will do, Joanne!'

The two women spoke in unison, and Kate felt an added twinge of anxiety at her daughter's words. 'You never did tell me what he said to you,' she added tautly. 'Or how you came to speak to a man you didn't know.'

Joanne pulled a face. 'Honestly, talk about the inquisition! I met him, right? I was hanging about at the gates when he drove in. He asked me what I was doing, and I told him I was looking for you. He gave me a ride down to the stables, and that's it.'

'You got into his car?' exclaimed her grandmother in an appalled tone, and Joanne looked to her mother for support.

'You knew that,' she said. 'And you didn't say anything about it.'

'Because I thought at first that his little girl was with him,' put in Kate shortly. 'And you don't need me to tell you my views about accepting lifts from strange men.'

'He isn't a strange man. He's your boss,' protested Joanne indignantly. She flung herself off her chair. 'In any case, I think he's really nice.' Her jaw jutted. 'He talked to me. He really talked to me, you know? Like I was an adult, not some dumb kid!'

'I don't talk to you like you're a dumb kid,' objected her mother at once, wondering what Alex Kellerman could have said to evoke this kind of response from her daughter. 'And—' she cast her mother a hopeful look '—perhaps we are overreacting a little bit. You were on Mr Kellerman's land, after all.'

'Even so…' began Ellen Ross, but Joanne wasn't listening to her.

'You do like him, don't you?' the young girl asked, giving her mother a sly look. 'I could tell.'

'You're talking nonsense!' exclaimed Kate hotly, plunging her hands into the soapy water in an effort to avoid any further discussion of Alex Kellerman. 'Come on. You can dry. Your grandmother can go and sit down for once.'

But later that evening, after Joanne had gone to bed, Ellen Ross returned to the subject of Kate's temporary employer. 'I still think taking a job at Jamaica Hill was going too far,' she declared. 'You don't really know anything about that man, and I don't like the idea that he's influencing Joanne now. How do you know he wasn't responsible for his wife's death? Somebody had to have put those horses into the wrong stalls, so why not him?'

Kate sighed. 'I think if Alex Kellerman had wanted to kill his wife he'd have chosen a more certain way of doing it,' she replied quietly.

'What do you mean?'

'Oh, Mum.' Kate shook her head. 'You know as well as I do that the chances of someone being killed by a fall from a horse are fairly slim. People fall from horses all the time without any serious injury. Or she could have been paralysed, brain-damaged, even. Neither of which would have achieved what he's supposed to have wanted to achieve.'

'Since when have you become such an expert?' asked her mother huffily. 'It seems to me that both you and Joanne have been taken in by Alex Kellerman's "sexy" manner.' She used her fingers to denote the quotation marks, and then grimaced. 'Well, just be careful, Kate. You're not infallible and Alex Kellerman is a very clever man.'

Didn't she know it?

But Kate made no comment. She preferred not to have to explain her own reasons for thinking so to her mother and the knowledge that what the older woman had said was probably true didn't help. Not least that despite what she'd heard—and the warnings she'd given herself—she still found her employer an intriguing enigma. Not sexually attractive, she assured herself, but fascinating nonetheless.

Kate went into her office early the next morning.

She made a point of calling in at the agency every two or three days to read her messages and check the post. Susie wasn't in that early, of course, and she and Kate usually kept in touch by phone. For the time being, Susie was in nominal charge of the office, and she had orders to try and postpone any enquiries and sign cheques for any service bills that came due in her employer's absence.

Today, Susie had left a couple of letters for her attention. One of them was from the insurance company who generally used her services in their inquiries, asking if she was free to accompany their assessor on a visit to see a claimant in Bath. The other was from the garage that serviced the Vauxhall, reminding her that it was due for its next road test at the end of the month.

More expense, thought Kate gloomily, appalled at how much of the two thousand pounds Henry Sawyer had given her she'd already spent. She'd earned some of it, of course, but she doubted he would think she was any further forward, and playing fencing games with Alex Kellerman wasn't getting her anywhere.

She studied the letter from Lingard's Life Assurance one more time before scribbling a note refusing the offer for Susie to type up when she came in. She thought ruefully that she would have liked nothing better than to be able to accept such an undemanding job. But insurance investigations didn't usually pay very large dividends, and in any case she was committed to her present client for the next two weeks at least.

She decided the letter from the garage could wait until later. Despite its age, the car was running reasonably efficiently at the moment, even if it did spend all its days and nights in the open air. When her father was alive, and they'd all shared the house in Edgecombe Crescent, it had enjoyed the luxury of a garage. But the apartments where they now lived provided only parking spaces, and Kate had had to invest in an alarm to protect the car.

She checked to see that there were no further messages on the answering machine, and then, after straightening the papers on her desk, she walked reluctantly towards the door.

But she paused and took a last wistful look around the office.
She missed the familiarity of these surroundings, she thought.
She missed the anticipation of what each new day would
bring. But most of all she missed being herself. She simply
wasn't cut out to live a lie.

Which was defeatist talk, she chided herself severely as
she rattled down the stairs again and crossed the street to
where she'd left the car. She was letting the slow progress
she was making influence her thinking, when it took time to
gain the confidence of her fellow employees. She had to find
a way to talk to Billy Roach again. She was fairly sure he
knew more about Alicia Sawyer's disappearance then he'd
said. But, first of all, she had to see Mr Guthrie and ask him
for some time off this morning. She doubted he'd be very
pleased to hear that she was a single mother, let alone that
she was going to have to try and find some way to explain
her daughter's misdemeanours to her head teacher.

Her confidence received something of a blow when she
arrived at Jamaica Hill to find Alex Kellerman's mud-
spattered Range Rover parked at the stables. She looked
about her rather apprehensively as she pulled into the space
beside the other vehicle. But to her relief there was no sign
of her employer. Only Billy, and one of the other apprentices,
hosing down the yard.

She acknowledged their greetings, but now was not the
time to look for answers. She guessed Kellerman was with
Sam Guthrie, and until he left her request would have to wait.
It was just her hard luck that he'd chosen to visit the stables
this morning. Still, she had plenty of time. Her appointment
with Mr Coulthard was not until ten o'clock.

When she opened her office door, a pleasing wave of
warmth enveloped her. It was a bright morning, but it was
cold, and she was glad Mr Guthrie had remembered to turn
on her fire. He didn't always do so and sometimes the room
felt as cold as charity. She hoped it was an omen. He must
be in a good mood.

She had loosened her tweed jacket and was unwinding the

green chenille scarf from her neck when Mr Guthrie's office door opened. Half expecting it to be Alex Kellerman, Kate managed not to look too dismayed when he appeared. At least he was leaving, which was good news. But although she waited for Mr Guthrie to follow him out Alex appeared to be alone.

'Good morning,' he said, his lean dark face far too knowledgeable for her liking. 'I thought you'd like to know that Sam won't be coming in today. His wife rang to say he's not feeling so good.' He shrugged his shoulders. 'She thinks he might be getting the flu.'

Oh, great!

Kate knew an immediate—and selfish—feeling of frustration. But she couldn't help wishing that the old man hadn't chosen today of all days to be ill. She sighed impatiently. What was wrong with her? No one *chose* to be ill. It just happened.

'Something wrong?'

Alex was watching her closely, and Kate made a pretence of folding her scarf and putting it on her desk. But her mind was buzzing with the realisation that she would have to ask him if she wanted to take part of the morning off.

'Not really,' she said now, stopping short of taking off her jacket. 'Um—I hope he'll be feeling better soon.'

'Don't we all?' But Alex's green eyes had narrowed. 'Until then, you'll have to put up with me, I'm afraid.'

Kate forced a polite smile, and turned away to put her bag in the desk drawer. It was only when she straightened that she was reminded that she was wearing a short skirt this morning. She'd dressed more formally than usual to go and see Joanne's headmaster and her careless action had exposed a provocative length of thigh.

The urge to try and pull down the hem of her skirt was almost irresistible, even though her long legs were encased in warm black tights. Then she met his sensual gaze, and she was fairly sure that he knew what she was thinking. Her skin prickled with an awareness she didn't want to admit.

'Did you talk to Joanne?'

His question was so at odds with the way he'd been looking at her that for a moment Kate couldn't think what he meant. But then the audacity of his enquiry hit her, arousing a sense of outrage she was able to channel into keeping her unwelcome attraction to him at bay.

'I—whether or not I spoke to my daughter is hardly relevant, Mr Kellerman,' she declared stiffly. 'And if she turns up here again I'd be grateful if you'd remind her that this is my place of work.'

Alex's dark brows arched. 'In other words, mind my own business,' he remarked tightly. 'Okay. If that's what you want. I wouldn't like to be accused of attempting to corrupt a minor as well as everything else.'

Kate sighed. 'I'm not accusing you of attempting to corrupt her.'

'No?' He raked one hand through his overlong hair. 'It sounded like it to me.'

'Well, I wasn't.' She took a breath. 'It's just—complicated, that's all.' Then, deciding that it might as well be now as later, she said, 'As a matter of fact, I was going to ask Mr Guthrie if I could have a couple of hours off this morning. I—I have to go to Lady Montford, you see.'

'I assume you mean Joanne's school?'

Kate gripped the edge of her desk. 'That's right. I have to see her head teacher.'

Alex grimaced. 'Well, I must say you have a hell of a way of asking for a favour,' he remarked dryly. 'And at the risk of being accused of interfering again, is there anything I can do?'

Kate's shoulders sagged. 'I don't think so, thank you.' But it was kind of him to ask. She swallowed. 'My appointment's at ten o'clock. Would it be all right if I left about half-past nine?'

Alex frowned. 'If you think that will give you sufficient time.' He paused. 'I suppose Joanne is going with you?'

Kate looked up. 'What makes you think she's not in school?'

Alex lifted his shoulders. 'Call it intuition,' he responded flatly. He massaged the back of his neck with a weary hand. 'You can go whenever you want.'

'Thanks.' But Kate still regarded him warily. 'Um—what exactly did Joanne say to you?'

'Do you expect me to betray a lady's confidence?' he mocked her gently, his hand falling to his side. 'Besides, it isn't—relevant—is it?'

Kate slumped. 'She told you, didn't she?'

'What?' He gave her an innocent look and she wanted to scream.

'Why—why she wanted to see me!' she exclaimed at last, gazing at him frustratedly. 'Why I have to see her head teacher this morning.' She groaned. 'That's why you told me to go easy on her. God, you must think I'm such a fool!'

'I don't think you're a fool, Kate.' He abandoned his stance beside the door into the manager's office and came further into the room. 'As a matter of fact I have nothing but admiration for you. You're doing a great job. It can't have been easy bringing up a child on your own.'

'No.' Kate blew out breath. 'No, it hasn't been,' she conceded ruefully, trying not to feel threatened because he was now standing just an arm's length away. But in black jeans and a dark green corded jacket he was disturbingly familiar. It was odd how in such a short time she had come to know his appearance so well.

'That's what I thought.'

There were waistline pockets in his jeans and now he hooked his thumbs inside them, drawing her attention to the powerful thighs they enhanced. Reminded her, too, of his sexuality, and the not unimpressive bulge against his zip.

God!

She was horrified at where her thoughts were leading her. She had to remember that he was the man she had come here to investigate. She must be crazy to be entertaining any ideas about his masculinity when his relationship to the missing woman was still in doubt.

'Would you like to talk about it?'

She realised suddenly that he'd misinterpreted her silence. He'd assumed she was still worrying about Joanne when her daughter's problems had been far from her thoughts. She wondered what he'd say if she told him she'd been speculating about his sexual preferences. He was a sensual man; there had to be some woman in his life.

'Talk about what?' she asked now, buying a little time, and a look of resignation crossed his face.

'What indeed?' he countered quietly, turning back towards Mr Guthrie's office. 'Let me know when you're leaving. I'll have all calls switched through to me.'

'No—wait—' Kate went after him, stopping herself just short of grabbing his arm. 'That is, I'll tell you what happens when I get back.' She bit her lip. 'If you're interested.'

'I am,' he agreed gently. 'Good luck.'

When the door closed behind him, she filled her lungs completely for the first time since he'd come into her office. What was there about him, she wondered, that put every nerve in her body on red alert? When she was near him, she was conscious of herself in a way she'd never experienced before. No wonder Alicia had been infatuated with him—if she had, she amended swiftly. It was far too easy to jump to the wrong conclusions where he was concerned.

Deciding there wasn't much point in starting anything until she got back, Kate decided to take him up on his offer and make an early start. With a bit of luck, she should be back by eleven o'clock, and she'd make sure she caught up on all her correspondence before she went home.

But, as she wrapped her scarf around her neck again, she knew she was being rather optimistic. She had no idea how long the interview with Mr Coulthard might take, and the thought that Joanne could end up with a suspension from school, or worse, filled her with apprehension.

Lifting her bag out of the drawer again, she crossed to the

door leading into Mr Guthrie's office. Tapping lightly on the panels, she waited until Alex answered before putting her head around the door. 'I'm leaving now,' she said, when he looked up from the stock book. 'I've switched the phones through to you. Is that okay?'

'Okay.'

Alex nodded, and Kate closed the door again and started for the door. So far, so good, she thought, trying to be optimistic. All she had to do now was pick up Joanne, which would give her plenty of time to cope with the morning traffic.

The old Vauxhall looked more shabby than usual beside the Range Rover. Alex's vehicle might need a wash, but even dirty it possessed a powerful appeal. Much like its owner, reflected Kate as she slid behind the wheel of her own car. Her lips twitched. Not that she was in any position to judge.

Nevertheless, as she turned the key in the ignition, she had to admit that the night's growth of beard on his jaw this morning had suited him. He'd obviously left the house in a hurry after learning that Mr Guthrie wasn't going to be in that day. The car hiccupped, but didn't start, and she stifled an expletive. She had to stop thinking about Alex Kellerman so personally and concentrate on why she was here.

She tried to start the car again, but once again it refused to respond to her efforts. And, no matter how she tried to coax it into action, the engine simply wouldn't fire. 'Oh, great,' she muttered irritably. This was all she needed. She would have to go and call a taxi now and hope that one could get here in time.

She'd attracted the attention of a couple of the hands who worked at the stables, but before one of them could come and offer his help the office door opened and Alex himself came out. At once, the other men reverted to what they'd been doing, and Kate thrust open her door and got out of the car as her employer strolled across the yard.

'I won't ask if you're having problems, because I can see

you are,' he remarked without sarcasm. 'What's wrong? Have you flooded the carburettor, or what?'

'You tell me,' muttered Kate frustratedly. 'I just know it won't start.'

'Let me try.' Alex got into the car and flicked the ignition. But although the engine turned over a couple of times it remained obstinately uncooperative. 'I think it may be flooded,' he said at last, getting out again. 'Would you like me to get my mechanic to take a look at it? In the meantime, I could give you a lift into town.'

Kate thought ruefully of the letter she'd read that morning. If she'd kept up to date with the car's maintenance, this might never have happened. 'Um—well, if you could give me a lift to the taxi rank at the bus station, I'd be grateful,' she acknowledged weakly. 'But I'll get the garage where it's serviced to come and collect the car.'

Alex shrugged. 'If you like.' He paused. 'But it's possible they'd have a wasted journey. If it is flooded, it will start again once the petrol's had time to evaporate, you know.'

Kate hesitated. There was no doubt that she could do without another bill if it wasn't necessary. 'Well—if your mechanic doesn't mind,' she murmured awkwardly, wondering what her father would have done in a case like this.

But, of course, her father would never have got himself into a situation like this, she conceded, after Alex had closed the office door and unlocked the Range Rover so that she could get in. He'd never have become involved with someone he was investigating, let alone got himself into a position where he was indebted to the man himself.

'Right.' Alex climbed into the vehicle beside her, and she was instantly aware of how much she wanted to believe he was innocent of the charge she was investigating. In the confined space of the car, she couldn't help inhaling the clean male scent of his body, the piney scent of his aftershave lingering so pleasantly on his skin that she almost started when he spoke again. 'Do you want to remind me of your address?'

'My address?'

'I assume you want to collect your daughter before going to the school?'

'Well, yes.' Kate swallowed. 'But there's no need for you to take us. If you'll drop me at the taxi rank, I can take it from there.'

Alex gave her a sidelong glance as he reversed the powerful motor, and she wondered what he was thinking. But she could hardly explain that her apparent lack of gratitude was due to the fact that she didn't want him to see exactly where she lived. She'd had to give her address, of course, when she'd applied for the job at the stables, but she'd hoped he'd never have occasion to notice it himself.

'I'll take you to the school,' he said now, and she decided not to argue with him. After all, at least twenty other families lived in the block of flats where she and her family lived. Unless he checked, he'd never know there wasn't a Hughes among them. That there was a Ross could surely mean nothing to him.

'Well—if you don't mind,' she murmured as they accelerated towards the gates.

'If I had, I wouldn't have offered,' he remarked sardonically. 'What's the matter? Are you afraid your boyfriend will find out I've been chauffeuring you around?'

'I don't have a boyfriend,' retorted Kate, without thinking, and she scolded herself for the lack of professionalism she'd displayed. If she wasn't careful, he'd trick her into revealing what she was really doing at the stables, and her nails dug into her palms at the prospect of what that would mean.

'Why not?' he asked, and she looked at him blankly. 'Why don't you have a boyfriend?' he amplified mildly, and she hurriedly looked away.

'I don't have time for men,' she said at last, staring out of the window. 'And I live in Milner Court. That's off Marlborough Road.'

'Okay.' Alex absorbed the information. Then, as if this was some game he liked to play, he said, 'Joanne's father must have hurt you very badly. Didn't you say she was little more than a baby when he died?'

Kate heaved a sigh, wishing she'd never confided in him. 'It was a long time ago,' she said dismissively. She clenched her fists. 'I suppose I could say the same about you,' she added, deciding he could hardly object if she answered in kind.

He was silent for a few moments, and she half thought he wasn't going to respond to her challenge. His expression had darkened, and his long fingers had tightened on the wheel. But then, with a shrug of his shoulders, he seemed to come to a decision. 'I hardly think my situation qualifies, do you?'

Kate took the opportunity he was offering. 'Why not?' she asked innocently, and he glanced her way, his thick lashes shadowing the expression in his eyes.

'What woman would trust herself with me after what I've been accused of?' he enquired dryly. 'Oh, no, Mrs Hughes, I'm in no doubt as to what most of your sex would think of me.'

'Well, I think you're exaggerating,' declared Kate swiftly, and a look of wry amusement crossed his face.

'And I think you're being charitable,' he countered. 'Let's talk about your daughter. That's a safer topic, don't you think?'

Kate shifted a little restlessly in her seat. She might never have another chance to talk to him like this. 'I'm sure there are plenty of women who'd like to get to know you,' she persisted. 'Who'd jump at the chance to visit Jamaica Hill.'

Alex expelled a resigned breath. 'Really?'

'Yes, really.'

'Why? So that they could say they'd seen the spot where the dastardly deed took place?'

'No.' Kate sensed that despite his mockery it still hurt him to talk about it, but she told herself she mustn't feel sorry for him. 'Are you telling me you haven't brought any other women to—to the house since your wife died?'

Alex's eyes narrowed. 'I don't think that's anything to do

with you, Mrs Hughes,' he responded harshly. 'Are you sure you're not working for someone else as well as me?'

Kate went cold. 'I don't know what you mean.'

'I mean my father-in-law, Mrs Hughes. Perhaps he can't get the answers he wants from my staff, so he's sent you.'

Kate gasped. 'I don't even know your father-in-law, Mr Kellerman,' she protested, glad she could be honest. 'And I can assure you, I'm not working for him.'

'Well, good.' His lips twisted. 'I believe you. I guess I'm just not good at answering questions any more.'

Kate managed to hide the relief she was feeling. For a moment there, she'd thought he'd guessed why she'd taken the job. But in his position she supposed he had to be careful what he said, and to whom. The case of how his wife had died was considered closed, but if any further evidence was forthcoming she supposed it could be opened again...

CHAPTER SIX

IT WAS after twelve o'clock by the time they got back to Jamaica Hill.

Although Kate had insisted that there was no need for him to wait, Alex had hung about the school gates for over an hour while she and Joanne had their interview with Mr Coulthard, Joanne's head teacher.

And it was just as well he had, Alex reflected now, glancing once again at Kate's white face. The head teacher had proved to be tough and intractable, and she had taken his decision badly. He also knew she blamed herself for Joanne's behaviour and no amount of persuasion on either his or Joanne's part would change her mind.

Joanne; herself, had proved surprisingly resilient, though Alex suspected she might behave somewhat differently in the privacy of her own room at home. But she seemed to realise how upset her mother was and in consequence she'd kept her own feelings to herself.

Alex admired her sensitivity, and after they'd dropped the girl at the flat he'd done his utmost to convince Kate that, far from letting her daughter down, she'd given her values anyone would admire. But he couldn't do anything about Joanne's suspension, or make Kate see that Mr Coulthard had really had no choice.

Now, he realised, he didn't want to return her to the office. Despite her assertion that she'd be better off at work, he was of the opinion that she needed a break. Her mother, whom he'd met briefly that morning, had suggested that he might be agreeable to giving her the rest of the day off, but although he had willingly concurred Kate had insisted on returning to the stables.

77

'Have lunch with me,' he offered abruptly as he swung the Range Rover between the stone gateposts, and Kate turned to give him a startled look.

'Lunch?' she echoed, and he nodded. 'Oh, really, that's not necessary. Um—I've got some biscuits in my office. That's all I need.'

Alex slowed the car. 'Is that what you usually have for lunch? Biscuits?'

'Well—no.' Kate moistened her lips. 'As—as a matter of fact, I usually get a sandwich from the van.' A firm from King's Montford delivered fresh sandwiches every morning, but of course today she hadn't been there when they came round.

'Then why not join me today?' Alex persisted, allowing the engine to idle. 'Mrs Muir will be glad to have someone to cater for, for a change.'

Kate drew a breath. She was hesitating, and Alex pressed his advantage. 'You can tell me what Coulthard's going to do about the other girls who were involved.'

Kate sighed. 'Are you really interested?'

'I am, as a matter of fact. I like Joanne.'

'And she likes you,' murmured Kate almost inaudibly, and then blushed when she realised he'd heard her. 'Well—if you're sure your housekeeper won't object.'

'It is my house,' Alex reminded her mildly, turning up towards the main building. He parked on the paved forecourt. 'Come on. You look as if you could use a drink.'

Mrs Muir appeared as they entered the large reception hall, where a Waterford crystal chandelier was suspended from the ceiling of the second floor. As the little woman came to meet them, he was aware of Kate looking about her with interest and for the first time in years he wondered what someone else thought of his home.

Agnes Muir was thin and angular, not at all the rosy-cheeked retainer so lovingly described in popular fiction. Yet, for all that, she was loyal, and she had a kind and generous nature, and it had hurt her very badly when Rachel was taken away.

'Och, there you are, Mr Kellerman!' she exclaimed, her eyes darting swiftly between them, and he guessed she was curious about why he'd brought Kate here. 'Mrs Sheridan's been on the phone half a dozen times this morning already. Didn't you promise her you'd go and look at her new colt?'

'Damn.' He'd forgotten all about Lacey's invitation, and he saw Kate turn to give him a doubtful glance. He should have rung Lacey before he left, but he'd been thinking of other things at the time. 'Not to worry,' he added reassuringly, more for Kate's benefit than his housekeeper's. 'If she rings again, I'll explain that I had to go out.'

'Very well.' Mrs Muir folded her hands at her waist, and he knew she was waiting for him to tell her where he'd been. Either that or introduce her to his companion, he conceded without rancour. Agnes had begun to consider herself the mistress of the house.

'If you'd rather—' began Kate awkwardly, and he realised she'd misunderstood his hesitation, probably imagining he would rather have kept his appointment with Lacey.

'I wouldn't,' he assured her, taking her arm to bring her forward, and then frowning when she jerked away.

But he had no time to consider that rejection, or what it might mean, and, keeping his temper in check, he introduced her to the housekeeper without delay. 'Mrs Hughes works with Sam, as you know,' he added, aware that his tone was clipped and formal. 'I've invited her for lunch. Is that a problem?'

'As if it would be!' exclaimed Agnes, evidently liking what she'd seen of Kate. 'If you'll give me thirty minutes, I'll have the meal ready for you.'

'Thanks.'

Alex knew his voice was curt, but he couldn't help it. He hadn't realised until then how much Kate's confidence in him had meant. But the way she'd pulled away, as if she was revolted by his touch, had dealt him quite a blow, and he wondered if she'd been fooling him all along.

The thought was repellent, and rather than allow it to fester he pushed it aside and led the way into the library, which was situated at the front of the house. The leather-bound volumes on the shelves were seldom moved, but the room was one of his favourites, the open fire in the huge hearth giving it a warmth and familiarity he normally enjoyed.

'What would you like to drink?' he asked, moving to a cabinet in the corner, where a selection of bottles and decanters occupied a silver tray. There was a built-in fridge below which Mrs Muir kept stocked with beer and mixers, despite her contention that Alex drank too much.

'Oh—just an orange juice, please.'

Kate was hovering in the entrance, and he wondered if she was afraid he might jump her if she closed the door. He might, too, he thought aggressively, if only to punish her for treating him like one of the untouchables, but then he saw her anxious face and his anger cooled.

'Orange juice,' he said, bending to swing open the door of the cool-box. He found what he wanted, flicked the tab, and poured the contents into a stemmed glass. 'Is that okay?'

'Thanks.'

She took the glass from him, but this time he made sure their fingers didn't touch. If she thought he'd invited her here for any ulterior motive, she could think again. He'd felt sorry for her, that was all. He'd have done the same for anyone.

Like Alicia...

He scowled. He didn't want to think about her now. He didn't want to remember how she'd deceived him, too. All that talk about her husband beating her; how she was too afraid to go on living at home. He should have put her in touch with social services or one of those hostels that catered for battered wives, instead of giving her temporary accommodation in his home.

The memory of how she'd duped him caused him to regard Kate with even less sympathy. What if she was only here to

see how much she could get out of him? He still wasn't
entirely satisfied she'd told him the truth about taking this
job.

'You've got a lovely home,' she murmured as he was
opening a bottle of beer for himself. 'Is—is the house very
old?'

'Parts of it date back to the seventeenth century,' he told
her coolly. He took a swig of beer from the bottle and wiped
the back of his hand across his mouth. 'Thankfully, my
grandfather decided to modernise the old place. Much as I
appreciate its history, it's bloody hard to keep it warm.'

Kate smiled. 'I love open fires, don't you?' she said, gesturing towards the logs burning in the grate. 'We just have
electric heating at the flat.'

Alex watched her. 'And you live there with your mother
and your daughter?'

'That's right. I couldn't have got—got a job without her
help.'

Now why did he think she had been going to say something other than that she'd been able to get a job? he wondered. There was no doubt that when Joanne was younger
she'd have needed a babysitter for the child. He lifted the
bottle to his lips and took another swallow. He was letting
his irritation at her edginess affect his mood.

'Why don't you sit down?' he suggested, gesturing towards an armchair nearer the fire, and although he was sure
she would have preferred to stand she moved to take the seat.

'I envy you all these books,' she remarked rather nervously, when he came to stand in front of the fire. 'I've
always loved books and reading.' She grimaced. 'I just wish
Joanne felt the same.'

Alex hesitated, and then, because he wasn't naturally aggressive, he subsided into the chair across the hearth. 'I
shouldn't worry,' he said, with rather more warmth. 'Maybe
being suspended will prove a godsend in the long run.'

'How can you say that?'

She wasn't prepared to be polite where her daughter was

concerned and Alex noticed how her eyes sparkled when she was provoked. He found himself wondering how she would look if he was making love to her. Would her mouth taste as hot and sensual as it looked right now?

'I mean,' he said mildly, 'it will give her time to consider her options, and if Coulthard's going to put her into a different class next term it will be like a new start.'

Kate hunched her shoulders. 'I suppose.'

'Well, he had to do something, Kate!' Alex exclaimed reasonably, and then cursed himself when her arching brows told him she'd noted the familiarity. 'Shoplifting is a serious offence,' he added, trying to cover himself. 'If he'd let her off, he'd have had to let the other girls off as well.'

'He doesn't know who the other girls are!' exclaimed Kate at once. 'Joanne refused to tell him.'

'Still, I'd say he has a fairly good idea,' retorted Alex shrewdly. 'He'll be watching them like a hawk. They won't get away with it for long.'

'I wish I could believe that,' muttered Kate, sipping her orange juice almost without thinking. 'But you're right. Joanne did deserve some punishment. I just wish I didn't feel so helpless.'

Alex rolled the bottle he was holding between his palms. 'At least you don't lie awake nights wondering what lies other people are telling her about you,' he said heavily. 'Believe me, that's the hardest thing to take.'

She frowned then. 'You're talking about your own daughter, aren't you?'

'Rachel. Yes.' Alex wondered again why he found it so easy to confide in her. 'You probably know that she lives with my in-laws. What you may not know is that they don't intend to give her up.'

Kate stared at him. 'Intend?' she said curiously. 'That's an odd word to use. Don't you mean they don't *want* to give her up?'

'I mean intend,' he told her grimly. 'Conrad Wyatt will do anything to stop me getting my daughter back.' He grimaced.

'I guess you could say I've been making it easy for him. For a while after Pamela died I hit the bottle pretty badly.'

Kate shook her head. 'That's understandable.'

'Is it?' Alex wished she'd been around then. He might have had more sense than to destroy what was left of his reputation. He scowled as the memories came flooding back. 'You can't imagine what it was like, being accused of killing my own wife.'

'No.'

Kate conceded the point, but there was no trace of censure in the word. On the contrary, she seemed almost willing to believe him. Or was he being absurdly naïve to think that?

'You said your husband was killed in a car crash,' he observed now, deciding he'd said enough about himself. 'That must have been tough on you.'

She stiffened at his words. He sensed it immediately, without the sudden straightening of her spine. He had evidently stepped into territory that was still painful to her, and he cursed himself for destroying their unexpected rapport.

'It was,' she told him tensely. 'I suppose you think it's because Joanne doesn't remember what it was like to have a father that she's so rebellious now.'

'I didn't say that,' he replied evenly. 'I was merely comparing your situation with mine.' He grimaced. 'At least no one has accused you of being responsible for the accident.'

Kate put down her glass. He sensed she would have liked to get to her feet and pace about the room, but perhaps the fear of what he might do deterred her. 'Perhaps I was,' she said at last. 'Responsible, I mean.' She pressed her knees together. 'If Sean had been happy with me, he wouldn't have gone off with someone else.'

Alex's expression was sympathetic. 'I doubt if it's as simple as that,' he remarked gently, and she gave him a rueful look.

'You'll have gathered that I don't like to talk about Sean,' she murmured. 'It just reminds me of what a fool I was.' She paused. 'I should have listened to my parents. If it hadn't been for them I'd never have been able to finish my degree—'

'You've got a degree!' Alex was stunned, and, looking at her suddenly flushed face, he realised she hadn't intended to tell him that. But the words had just slipped out, and now she was stuck with them. 'A degree in what?' he demanded, trying not to feel suspicious. He filled his lungs. 'Not journalism, I hope.'

'Law,' she got out jerkily. 'I got a degree in law.' And then, seeing his scepticism, she added, 'It's true. But I couldn't find a firm of solicitors willing to take me on so, as I told you, I went to work for my father.'

Alex breathed deeply through his nostrils. Then he got abruptly to his feet. A degree in law, and she had taken a job at his stables. Was he being unnecessarily paranoid to wonder why?

He was staring out of the long windows when he realised she had come to stand beside him. Beyond the windswept gardens that surrounded the house, the land sloped away towards the river, and he noticed the lower meadow was partly flooded. They'd had so much rain in the last few weeks, it was to be expected, he supposed, trying to ignore her and not succeeding.

'I'm sorry if you think I should have told you,' she ventured, to attract his attention. 'I know I didn't put it on my CV, but that was because so many employers are put off by qualifications like that.'

Alex half turned towards her. 'And you thought I would have been one of them?' His lips twisted. 'You didn't want to embarrass an ignorant horse-trader like me?'

'You're not an ignorant horse-trader.'

His eyes narrowed. 'How do you know?'

She shifted a little uncomfortably. 'I should have thought it was obvious.' She took a breath. 'Ignorant people aren't usually sensitive, and—and you've just proved you are.'

'Am I?'

Alex knew it wasn't the most sensible thing to tease her,

but he was enjoying having her trying to placate him for a change. Besides which, he conceded tersely, she was a beautiful woman. Despite his self-derision, he was not entirely immune to the appeal in her grey eyes.

'You—you were kind to Joanne,' she told him firmly, turning her head slightly to avoid his gaze. A strand of crinkled hair fell forward and she looped it back behind her ears. 'I—I was glad you came with us today.'

'Yeah, so was I.'

Alex felt an instantaneous response to her admission, a recognition that his own motives hadn't been exactly impartial either. As she stood there beside him, the smell of her warm skin drifted irresistibly to his nostrils, a delicate fragrance that was overlaid by the sudden sharpness of his own desire.

God, he acknowledged darkly, he wanted to touch her. He didn't care at that moment who she was or what she'd done, he only wanted to ease her jacket off her shoulders and slide his sweating palms into the demure neckline of her shirt. What would she do? he wondered. How would she react if he took her small, high breasts into his hands? He wanted to see her eyes widen as he caressed them and squeezed them. Would her nipples be taut? Would they swell like hard buds against his palms?

'So—so I'm forgiven?'

When she spoke, he had to pull himself together before he could answer her. His head was swimming, and he hoped to hell she didn't look below his waist. 'Forgiven?' he echoed thickly, and she must have thought it was safe to turn her head and look at him, but when she met his burning gaze the hectic colour rose hotly into her cheeks.

'For—for not telling you about my degree,' she got out jerkily, clearly disturbed by his appraisal, and he remembered why he'd felt he needed some time to think about what she'd said. 'Um—why—why don't you tell me about your daughter?' she added hurriedly. 'I—I expect you miss her a lot.'

Alex blew out a breath. He wondered if it was only his

imagination that made him think she looked guilty, or was it fear that had brought such a look of agitation into her face? But one thing he did know: he didn't want to talk about Rachel right now. There would be something almost profane in using his daughter to dispel the way he felt.

'Are you afraid of me?' he asked abruptly, and this time he was not mistaken when she drew away.

But, 'No,' she said tensely, though her voice was slightly higher than before. 'Why should I be afraid of you, Mr Kellerman? I—I hardly know you.'

Alex couldn't let it go. 'Oh, I think you do,' he insisted softly, aware that his efforts to get rid of his own unwilling attraction weren't working. 'Know of me, at least,' he appended, moving closer. 'Perhaps you're beginning to wonder if there was any truth in the rumours. Do you think you're woman enough to find out?'

He heard the catch in her breath as she backed away from him. 'I think you're just amusing yourself at my expense, Mr Kellerman,' she said, forcing a valiant smile. But the smile didn't reach her eyes, and he realised she was still apprehensive. 'Shall we go and sit down again? I haven't finished my drink.'

Her efforts to reason with him didn't please him, however, they annoyed him. For God's sake, she was behaving as if he'd stepped out of line and it was up to her to rap his knuckles and send him back. Did she really think he was deceived by her pathetic attempts to appear sophisticated? If she'd had any sense, she'd never have left her seat.

'You know what I think?' he drawled now as she came up against the bookshelves. She'd been so intent on putting some distance between them that she hadn't realised she'd backed into a corner. 'I think you are afraid of me, Miss Hughes.' He lifted his hand and stroked her cheek with a carefully controlled finger. 'Don't be. I'm not half as dangerous as I look.'

She tilted her head away from his hand. 'I don't think you are dangerous,' she retorted recklessly. 'I think you're rather sad, if you want the truth. You've lost your wife; you've lost your child; you've lost your reputation. Why should I be afraid of someone who's just given up?'

'Damn you, I haven't given up!' Her words caught him on the raw, and he was furious with her for saying them. Without really thinking about what he was doing, he grabbed her shoulders in a savage grasp. 'You know nothing about me,' he snarled, forgetting that just minutes before he'd maintained the opposite. 'I should break your bloody neck for that remark!'

It wasn't until the words were out that he realised what he was saying, that she was bound to associate the threat with his wife's death. She probably thought he was capable of anything if he could lose his temper so easily, and Pamela had done a hell of a lot more than provoke him about his life.

But, by then, it was too late. Too late to withdraw his careless words; too late to wish he'd never started this; too late to ignore the woman beneath his hands. She was so warm, so feminine, so everything he'd been trying to shut out of his mind since she'd walked into his house, and, ignoring her stunned expression, he pulled her into his arms.

It was a mistake; a big mistake. He knew that as soon as he felt her yielding body against his own. Looking down into her wide, dilated eyes, he knew she was incapable of fighting him and although her fists were balled against his midriff it was a token gesture at best.

'I have not given up,' he repeated harshly, making one last attempt to bring some sanity into the situation, but she only shook her head. Whether she believed him or not, she expected him to exercise some restraint, but Alex found he couldn't let her go.

Instead, he bent his head to brush the pale curls of hair that nestled at her temples with his lips. She had secured her hair in a braid today, probably to try and impress the head teacher at Joanne's school with her severity, but several unruly strands had broken free and now clustered about her

face. Her hair was soft and tasted of her skin and his senses
spun in dizzying circles. He knew it was becoming impossible to let her go without tasting the dewy softness of her
mouth.

He thought she sensed what he was going to do before he
did it. Which was why her lips were pressed so tightly together when he sought her mouth with his. She was determined not to give in to him, even though he could feel her
trembling, and he despised himself for frightening her this
way.

But he didn't stop. He couldn't stop. Some inner hunger
was driving him on, and with one arm lodged securely about
her waist he brought his free hand to her face.

His thumb brushed her clamped lips, feeling their instinctive stiffening at the intimate caress. The tips of his fingers
probed her ear, finding the sensitive hollow beneath the soft
lobe, registering her rapidly beating pulse. She was all
woman, all warmth, all sanity, and he wouldn't have been
human if he hadn't been aware of it, and of the desire he had
to make her respond to him in return.

When his thumb found the curve of her chin and tilted her
face up to his, he could see the raw uncertainty in her expression, and it drove him on. Although she said nothing to
encourage him, he sensed that she was weakening, and he
wanted her to tell him how she felt.

'You don't hate me, do you, Kate?' he asked roughly,
bringing his other hand to cup her face between his palms.
'Believe me, I won't hurt you.'

'Won't you?'

There was still a trace of doubt in her voice, but her parted
lips were too much of an invitation for him to resist. She was
in his arms, he wanted her, and he lowered his head and
fastened his mouth to hers.

Alex's head swam. It was heaven and it was hell. Heaven
in the sensuous sweetness of her lips and hell in the knowledge that he could never have her. Why didn't she stop him?
he wondered frustratedly. Why didn't she fight him with

every scrap of strength she had? He was giving her the opportunity. Hell, he was as vulnerable as a schoolboy in his
present position.

But, when he permitted his tongue to slip between her
teeth, it met no obvious opposition. The moist hollow of her
mouth lay open to his eager assault, and his hands were not
entirely steady as they slid the jacket from her shoulders and
moved down her spine to clutch the slender contours of her
hips.

Another mistake. When he thrust his leg between hers to
bring her closer to him, he felt his hardness digging into her
soft stomach. The feeling was indescribable, and he wanted
desperately to ease his male arousal in her woman's body.

Her shirt had come free of the waistband of her skirt and
his fingers sought the silky heat of her bare skin almost without his volition. His palms spread against the smooth flesh
of her back before seeking a more intimate exploration. The
clip of her bra was no obstacle and then, taking a shuddering
breath, he allowed his thumbs to caress the undersides of her
breasts.

Suddenly, he couldn't breathe, and, releasing her mouth,
he buried his hot face in the scented hollow of her neck.
God, he must be crazy, he thought unsteadily. Not for the
first time, he was in danger of making a complete hash of
things. Did she have any idea what she was doing to him?
Did she realise how close to losing it he was? Perhaps she
did, he mocked himself derisively. Perhaps that was what he
could see in the sensual mystery of her gaze.

The sound of the door opening behind him brought him
partially to his senses. Agnes Muir, he thought bitterly. She
never had learned to knock before barging in.

Straightening, he barely glanced at Kate's flushed face before swinging round to confront his housekeeper. Only it
wasn't his housekeeper, he saw at once. It was Lacey
Sheridan, and she was staring at him with a look of harsh
contempt on her face.

'Well, well,' she said, whatever pain she might have felt

quickly concealed beneath a mask of sarcasm. 'And I thought you'd have learned your lesson by now.'

'Lacey,' he groaned frustratedly, shaking his head, but before he could offer any words, whether of protest or explanation, he had to save himself as Kate brushed past him, almost knocking him over in the process.

'Excuse me,' she muttered, though he doubted she meant it, and, draping the jacket she had snatched off the floor about her shoulders, she barrelled out into the hall.

'Kate! Wait!' he yelled, starting after her, but before he could catch up with her she had let herself out of the front door.

'I don't think the lady's interested,' remarked Lacey mockingly from behind him, curving a detaining hand over his shoulder. 'I'd advise you to let her go, darling.' And when he jerked away from her possessive touch her eyes narrowed maliciously as she added, 'You will if you want my continued support...'

CHAPTER SEVEN

'It's Mrs Hughes, isn't it?'

Kate had been trying to decide whether to put sausage or mince into her shopping basket when an unfamiliar voice accosted her. Or someone else, she acknowledged, glancing somewhat apprehensively around the supermarket. She turned to find Alex Kellerman's housekeeper regarding her with a mixture of wariness and doubt, and breathed a little easier when she saw there was no one else about.

'Mrs Muir.'

Kate's response assured the little woman she hadn't made a mistake, and her angular features creased into a smile. 'I thought it was you, Mrs Hughes,' she said warmly. 'I hope you're feeling better. Mr Kellerman explained how you had to rush away the other day.'

'Oh.' Kate's brain struggled to function. 'Oh, yes. I—I'm sorry about that.'

'No worries.' Mrs Muir patted her arm. 'Mrs Sheridan stayed for lunch instead. Still, it was a pity you and Mr Kellerman didn't have time to talk.'

'Oh—we talked,' murmured Kate wryly, a shiver at the memory of that conversation causing goosebumps down her spine. She wondered what Mrs Muir would have thought of her employer if it had been she who had interrupted them and not this Sheridan woman. 'Um—it's been nice seeing you again,' she added, hoping the diminutive Scotswoman would take the hint.

She didn't.

'You're managing all right on your own, are you? Down at the office, I mean,' she continued pleasantly. 'It was such a shame that Mr Kellerman had to go away this week. What with Sam Guthrie being off, and all. Though I've heard he's feeling much better than he was.'

'That's good news.' Kate expelled a cautious breath. 'And—and with Ted's help I'm managing fairly well.' Ted Lowes was the head groom, and Kate suspected he knew as much about the stables as anyone, although, like Mr Guthrie, he always referred to Alex as the boss.

'Do you have time to join me for a cup of tea?' Mrs Muir suggested now, indicating the small café that was owned by the supermarket. And then, as if thinking better of it, she shook her head. 'Och, it's after five. You've probably got things to do.'

Kate had. Lots of things, she thought ruefully, remembering the agency's accounts, which Susie had left for her that morning. Not to mention a rebellious teenager, who had too much time and too little to do, and her mother who had taken her granddaughter's suspension very badly.

But… She hesitated. She doubted there was anyone at Jamaica Hill who knew what went on better than Mrs Muir. 'Um—I'm not in a hurry,' she protested firmly. 'Thank you for inviting me.'

With her groceries packed into two carriers and stowed in the boot of her car, Kate joined Mrs Muir in the café. The older woman had already been served, Kate found, and now two individual pots of tea and two scones with butter and jam resided on the table she'd taken in the window.

'Isn't this cosy?' asked Mrs Muir happily, passing Kate a cup and saucer. 'I like to come in here, but I don't often have company. Since Mr Muir died, I don't find it so easy to make friends.'

'Oh, I'm sorry.' Kate was sympathetic. 'I know how hard it can be when—when a loved one dies.'

'Well, it has been almost two years,' said her companion, making a valiant effort to dismiss it. She started to butter one of the scones. 'Tell me about yourself. How long have you been married?'

'My husband's dead.' Kate had no wish to talk about herself, but she knew she couldn't get away with saying nothing. And, as Alex knew about Joanne... 'I do have a daughter, however. She'll be thirteen in a couple of months.'

'Thirteen!' Mrs Muir was obviously surprised. 'Why, you don't look old enough to have a daughter that age.'

'Well, it's very nice of you to say so, but I was nineteen when she was born,' said Kate dryly.

'Really?' Mrs Muir was impressed. 'Well, they say having a family keeps you young.'

'Don't you believe it,' murmured Kate, adding milk to her cup, and Mrs Muir put a hand up to her mouth.

'Oh, my!' she exclaimed. 'Here I am, asking you to have tea, and your daughter's probably waiting for you at home.' She shook her head apologetically. 'I'm afraid I didn't think. I hope she's more patient than my Jim used to be.'

'We live with my mother,' admitted Kate reluctantly, realising she was saying more than she'd intended. And then, because Mrs Muir still looked as if she was waiting, she said, 'My husband died in a car accident over ten years ago.'

'Oh, that's a shame.' Mrs Muir tutted. 'You must have been devastated, my dear. I hate to hear about young people getting killed. It's every parent's nightmare: burying a son or daughter.' She hesitated. 'My Jim was never the same, I know that.'

Kate's brows drew together. 'You've lost a child yourself?'

'Yes. Our son, Philip.' There were tears in Mrs Muir's eyes now, which made Kate feel even worse. She wondered if she was cut out for asking awkward questions, but the opportunity was too good to miss.

'I suppose the Wyatts must have felt that way when— when their daughter died,' she murmured carefully, and Mrs Muir pulled a tissue from her pocket.

'I can't speak for them,' she said shortly. 'I only know that they've made Mr Kellerman's life a misery. It wasn't his fault that Pamela broke her neck.'

'No.'

Kate didn't dare question her belief, but the housekeeper must have suspected that she wasn't convinced, because she went on, 'He's a good man, Mrs Hughes. He's been like a son to me. If it wasn't for him, I don't know where I'd have found the strength to go on.'

'When your husband died,' nodded Kate, but Mrs Muir wasn't finished.

'We keep each other company, Mr Kellerman and I,' she said, pushing the other scone towards Kate. 'He'll get the lassie back; I know he will. These things take time, that's all.'

Kate could have remarked that Alex Kellerman had had time, lots of it, but he'd apparently chosen to drown his sorrows in a bottle; but she didn't. Nevertheless, thinking of him and what he had done to her caused another prickle of apprehension to ripple through her veins. What might he have done if Mrs Sheridan hadn't interrupted them? What might *she* have done if that sensual assault had lasted any longer? She hated to admit it, but she had been weakening, the hungry urgency of his hands on her body driving all sane thoughts out of her head...

'Eat your scone,' urged Mrs Muir now, and Kate was obliged to break off a corner and spread the crumbling cake with butter. But she wasn't very hungry, her thoughts of Alex Kellerman leaving a bitter taste in her mouth.

Not that she'd seen him since that scene in the library at Jamaica Hill. As Mrs Muir had said, he'd been away for the past couple of days, and she was grateful. She didn't know what she'd have done if she'd had to face him the following morning. She'd been tempted to send a message pleading illness, but that had seemed such a cowardly thing to do.

All the same, she was being forced to view Henry Sawyer's accusations about Alex and his wife rather less sceptically. A man who would take advantage of someone he barely knew would not quibble over starting an affair with a woman who was actually living in his house. At least, that was the way she was beginning to see it—even if some small part of her shrank from pre-judging him this way.

'Anyway, how are you settling down at the stables?' Mrs Muir asked warmly. 'I know Sam Guthrie has no complaint about your work.' And then she abruptly turned to the subject Kate was struggling hard to find a way to broach. 'It's to be hoped you stay longer than the rest.'

'The rest?' Kate was hardly aware she was crumbling the rest of the scone until Mrs Muir pointed it out to her.

'The other girls who worked for Mr Guthrie,' she continued after Kate had dropped her hands into her lap. 'Of course, they weren't like you. They were fly-by-nights, most of them. The wages were never good enough, and as soon as something more lucrative came along off they'd go.'

Kate tried not to sound too interested. 'That's a shame,' she murmured casually. 'I expect Mr Guthrie got sick of having to train new staff.'

'Ay, well, I'm not saying he's an easy man to work with,' went on the housekeeper sagely. 'And his judgement isn't always what it should be.' She grimaced. 'But even Mr Kellerman was taken in by the last woman to do your job.'

Kate hesitated. 'Wasn't she any good?'

'She was a liar,' declared Mrs Muir staunchly. 'She told Mr Kellerman her husband used to beat her, and that wasn't true. It's obvious she only said it to gain his sympathy. She wanted to get into the house, that was all. She must have been planning it all along.'

'Planning what?'

Kate couldn't help the question, but Mrs Muir took a deep breath before she said, 'I really shouldn't be discussing it. It's Mr Kellerman's business, not mine.' She paused, and smiled at her companion. 'All I will say is that I'm glad Mr Guthrie's found a decent assistant at last.'

Kate almost groaned aloud. For a few moments, she'd actually believed she was making some progress, that Mrs Muir might hold the key to everything she wanted to know. But now all she felt was frustration, and the guilty knowledge of her own deception that wouldn't go away.

'Kate! Hi! How are you? Long time, no see.'

Kate had been so sunk in depression that she hadn't noticed the woman who had come up to their table and she was immediately reminded that there were worse things than losing out on a hot lead. Marian Garvey was someone she'd known while she was at university, someone who'd known she was working with her father, and who might conceivably blow her cover.

But, to her relief, Mrs Muir seemed grateful for the interruption. Perhaps she'd decided she'd said more than she should, Kate reflected ruefully. In any event, when Kate returned the other woman's greeting, Mrs Muir gathered together her bags and got to her feet.

'I'd better be going,' she said. 'Mr Kellerman will be wondering where I've got to. Goodnight, Mrs Hughes. I've enjoyed our little chat. Perhaps we'll see one another again next week.'

Kate managed a polite rejoinder, but when Marian dropped into the seat Mrs Muir had vacated, and said, 'A client?' she wished she'd made an excuse to leave, too.

'Just someone I know,' she murmured, using her teacup to hide any embarrassment Marian might see in her face. 'Her husband died quite recently. I was just keeping her company, that's all.'

'How charitable,' remarked Marian sardonically, regarding Kate with a faintly jaundiced eye. 'But did I hear her say *Mr Kellerman*? She's no relation of the notorious Alex, is she?'

'No.' Kate was defensive, but then, realising it wouldn't be wise to get into a discussion about her employer, she changed the subject. 'How are you, Marian? You're looking well.'

'Thanks.'

Marian took the compliment complacently, and in actual fact Kate had to admit that she hadn't changed a lot since their college days. She'd put on some weight, but she was fairly tall so she could carry it. However, Kate had always found her rather supercilious and far too inquisitive about other people's affairs.

'Well, I'd better be going, too,' Kate said awkwardly, hoping to avoid any further questions about herself. But when Marian stood up as well her heart sank.

'I'll come with you,' Marian declared, accompanying her to the exit. 'The store's so busy on Fridays. You can never get what you want.'

'Oh—but you haven't had your tea,' protested Kate, gesturing towards the self-service counter.

'I don't want any,' replied Marian, looping the strap of her bag over her shoulder. 'I only came into the café because I saw you. It's such an age since we've had a gossip.'

'Oh.'

Kate managed to hide her dismay, but there was no way of escaping her until they reached the car park. 'How's your daughter?' she asked, tucking her arm through Kate's as if they were bosom friends. 'Joanne. She must be—what? Twelve or thirteen now.'

Kate frowned. 'She's nearly thirteen,' she conceded, not sure where this was leading. 'She's very well, thank you. I expect your little boy is growing up, too.'

'Bobby, yes.' Marian dismissed her son almost carelessly. 'But imagine, Joanne's almost a teenager. I bet she's quite a handful, isn't she?'

Kate sucked in her breath. She was beginning to see where this was heading. 'Joanne's okay,' she said as they reached the revolving doors. 'It was good of you to ask.'

'Well, I know what teenagers are like,' said Marian, accompanying her outside. 'My Bobby may be too young yet, but my younger sister's at Lady Montford, you know.'

Like Joanne.

She didn't say the words, but she might as well have done. It was obvious Marian knew about Joanne's suspension and had decided to gloat. Kate supposed she should be grateful for the distraction, but she resented the sly way Marian had brought it up.

'How's Marcus?' she asked casually. 'I saw his picture in the newspaper just last week. You must be very proud of him.'

She omitted to mention the fact that she already knew that Marian and Marcus were divorcing. It was cruel, perhaps, reminding the other woman of her ex-husband's success as an entrepreneur, but she deserved the dig. Kate might be disappointed in Joanne herself, but that was her business. She'd do anything to protect her daughter from Marian's gossiping tongue.

'Marc and I split up some time ago,' Marian eventually told her tightly. 'But we're fine. Bobby's nearly six.' She seemed to recover her composure as they walked out into the car park. 'I can hardly believe it. But I imagine having a child of Joanne's age makes you feel quite old, aside from anything else.'

'Positively ancient,' agreed Kate, refusing to accept the challenge. She paused a moment, waiting to see which way Marian was heading before turning in the opposite direction. Then, after turning up the collar of her coat, she raised a hand in farewell. 'Take care,' she added pleasantly, and walked away.

In fact, Marian's car was parked practically next to the old Vauxhall, and Kate had to wait several minutes for the woman to drive away. She was shivering by the time she'd unlocked the car and got behind the wheel, and she reflected that it would serve her right if the car refused to start.

Thankfully, it didn't. Since Alex's mechanic had checked it out, she'd had no more trouble with it. According to the note he'd left sellotaped to the steering wheel, he couldn't find anything wrong with it. She'd evidently flooded the carburettor as Alex himself had said.

Nevertheless, she was in no mood to humour her daughter when she got home and found Joanne moping about the house. She had only herself to blame if she was bored, she told her shortly, ignoring her mother's look of warning, and Joanne muttered something under her breath before flouncing into her room.

'That wasn't very kind, Kate,' murmured Ellen Ross, helping her daughter unpack the groceries from the carrier bags. 'It isn't easy for her, spending all day cooped up in the flat.'

'And whose fault is that?'

Kate refused to let her mother make her feel guilty, and Ellen Ross's nostrils flared with sudden irritation. 'And you're not letting her forget it, are you? Not for a minute. Despite the fact that if it hadn't been for Joanne you'd have known nothing about it. Nor Mr Coulthard, either, though I suppose he was only doing his job. She could have gone on doing what the other girls were doing, but she didn't. You should be thankful she's not into drug-taking or something like that.'

Kate heaved a sigh. 'I should have known you'd take her side.'

'I'm not taking her side.' Ellen was indignant. 'I'm just trying to make you see that Joanne's not a bad girl, whatever you think.'

'I know.' Kate shook her head. 'Oh, I suppose I'll have to apologise. But, honestly, it's not been an easy day for me either.'

'Why?' Her mother regarded her with interest. 'Has something happened? I thought Mr Kellerman was away.'

'He is.' Kate hoped her mother would put the slight deepening of colour in her cheeks down to exertion. 'But I saw Marian Garvey in the supermarket. She couldn't wait to let me know she knew about Joanne.'

'I see.' Ellen looked thoughtful. 'Of course. The Westons' younger daughter goes to Lady Montford, too.'

'Yes.' Kate grimaced. 'I wouldn't be surprised if the whole town knows our business by now.'

'Stop exaggerating.' Kate's mother was philosophical. 'I doubt if anyone's interested in Joanne's suspension but us.

She's not unique, Kate. I'm sad to say that being suspended these days is quite a common punishment.'

Kate finished putting the frozen items into the freezer and then propped her hips against the cupboard. 'I suppose you're right.'

'I am.' Ellen held her daughter's gaze for a moment and then looked away. 'So why do I get the feeling you're still on edge?'

Kate blew out a breath. 'I'm not on edge.'

'Of course you are.' Ellen was impatient. 'We've lived together too long, Kate. I always know when you've got something on your mind. What is it? You've been like this since you came home on Wednesday afternoon.'

Kate turned back to the counter. 'You're imagining things.'

'No, I'm not. What did Mr Kellerman say after you'd dropped Joanne off at the flat?' She paused, and when Kate still didn't speak she made a terse sound of frustration. 'I thought when he let you off early that he'd understood how you felt.'

Kate sighed. 'He did.'

'And you say he's been away for the past couple of days, so it can't be anything he's done.' She sighed. 'Oh, well, if you don't want to tell me, I'll have to assume it's me.'

Kate groaned. 'Give it a rest, Mum, please. Nothing's happened, all right? I'm—just not sure where this case is leading, that's all.'

'You mean you think it's a waste of time?'

'Not exactly.'

'Then you do suspect that Alex Kellerman may be responsible for this woman's disappearance?' Her mother frowned. 'Oh, Kate, you will be careful, won't you?'

Kate shook her head. 'I don't know what I believe any more,' she said bleakly. She wrapped her arms about her midriff, as if to try and calm the churning nerves in her stomach. 'I—I think he may have had an affair with her. And if he did...'

'That doesn't make him a murderer,' argued Ellen practically. 'But I think you ought to tell Mr Sawyer what you've told me. It's not as if you're making any progress. Perhaps it is time you admitted defeat.'

It was a temptation to do as her mother suggested, but Kate ignored it. Despite what had happened, she was reluctant to give up her job at Jamaica Hill. She told herself it was because she'd made a start at gaining Mrs Muir's confidence, but the fact was that was very far from the truth.

'I'll give it another couple of weeks,' she said now, reaching for a bag of pasta. She split the Cellophane and dropped the contents into a pan. 'I thought we'd have spaghetti tonight,' she added, hoping her mother would take the hint. She didn't want to get into a long discussion about Alex Kellerman. She was far too unsure of the way she felt about him.

'Well, I think you're just filling in time until the money stops coming,' remarked Ellen reprovingly, but Joanne's reappearance from her bedroom prevented her from saying anything more. And Kate took the opportunity to make her peace with her daughter, thus evading any further discussion of the case.

The weekend passed much too quickly. Kate, who had spent Saturday and Sunday trying to avoid thinking about Alex Kellerman, had to summon all her courage just to get into the car and drive out to Jamaica Hill on Monday morning. Perhaps Mr Guthrie would be back, she cheered herself hopefully, and then was grateful when the traffic lights at the end of the high street turned to red at her approach.

Anything to delay her arrival at the stables, she thought ruefully, wondering how her employer would react when he saw her again. Perhaps he'd already thought of a reason to dismiss her, she reflected, and then chided herself for the hollow feeling that evoked inside her.

The trouble was, she'd started to like him, she conceded. It had been so kind of him to take her and Joanne to the school and then hang about until they came out. They'd both been grateful for his understanding, and when he'd invited her to have lunch with him she'd been happy to accept.

But that was when it had all started to unravel, she remembered. She'd been so edgy when he'd taken her arm to introduce her to the housekeeper that he'd got the idea that she was repulsed by his touch. If only he knew, she brooded tensely. It was because he disturbed her so much that she'd been forced to pull away.

It had proved impossible to rescue the situation after that. He'd been so tense when they first went into the library that it had been a struggle to keep any kind of conversation going. She'd wanted to talk about his daughter, but it had been difficult to find an opening, and then, when she had, she'd ruined it all by accusing him of giving up.

She cringed now when she recalled his anger, and the sarcasm he'd used to such good effect. By the time he'd yanked her into his arms, she'd been so bemused, she was shaking, and she'd have believed anything of him before he touched her mouth.

Kate was brushing her lips with a wondering finger when the sound of a horn behind her alerted her to the fact that the lights had changed. She put the car into gear and let the clutch out too fast so that the engine stalled. She was anxiously revving the Vauxhall's engine when the pock-faced youth in the car behind accelerated past.

Kate wished for a moment she had a powerful car that she could compete with, and then, kangaroo-ing across the junction, she chided herself again. She wasn't a youth, she reproved herself, she was a woman fast approaching middle age, with a pre-pubescent daughter to boot.

And allowing other road users to get up her back—literally—wasn't going to help her. She'd need a cool head if she was going to come out of the present situation with even an atom of self-respect. Because nothing could alter the fact that despite all her efforts to fight him off Alex had overcome her resistance. When Mrs Sheridan had walked in the door, Kate had been on the verge of kissing him back.

And he'd known it, damn him. That was why he'd come chasing after her when she'd grabbed her jacket and high-tailed it out of the door. Her only compensation was that she'd been too quick for him. She'd cut across the paddock to the stables, collected her car, and driven home.

Well—not immediately home, she amended as the stone gateposts that marked the entrance to Jamaica Hill hove into view. She'd had no desire to face her mother and daughter until she'd had time to recover from that sensual embrace, so she'd gone to the agency, sneaking into her office while Susie was out for lunch.

Of course she'd dreaded going to work the following morning, and she'd been so relieved to find Ted Lowes oc-cupying Mr Guthrie's desk. That was when he'd explained that the boss had accompanied Mrs Sheridan to Doncaster races, and that he wouldn't be back in the office until the following week.

Today?

Kate turned in at the gates with an involuntary shiver. She'd know soon enough if the Range Rover was parked down at the stables. It was, and her stomach clenched in protest. Oh, God, she thought, why hadn't she turned down his invitation to lunch?

Well, she hadn't, and she had to live with it. At least, until she'd satisfied herself that she'd done all she could to locate Alicia Sawyer. Someone must know something. The woman couldn't just disappear off the face of the earth. Perhaps to-day would be the day she'd get another chance to tackle Billy Roach. Despite her hopes about Mrs Muir, she sensed the young apprentice was more likely to be indiscreet than the housekeeper.

She parked her car and got out, brushing down the seams of her black woollen trousers and checking that her hair was neat before locking the door. She'd secured it in a French pleat today and she thought it looked satisfyingly business-like. She smoothed a couple of wisps behind her ears before setting off across the yard.

What could be so bad? she asked herself as two of the stable boys called a greeting. It was Kellerman who ought to be feeling ashamed of himself, not her. If he fired her, so what? She was hardly likely to take the case to an employees' tribunal. And Henry Sawyer could hardly complain if Alex threw her out.

This morning her office felt decidedly chilly. Unlike that other occasion, he hadn't bothered to turn on the fire in her room. With a tightening of her lips, she went across to attend to it, and then almost jumped out of her skin when Alex spoke behind her.

'Will you come into my office?' he asked, before she had time to bend down and flick the switch on the electric fire, and Kate schooled her nervous features before turning to face him. But she needn't have bothered. He'd already gone back into the other room, so her efforts to appear calm and composed were wasted. Still, she decided not to take off her fur-trimmed parka. It didn't look as if she was going to be there long enough for that.

He was standing behind Mr Guthrie's desk when she entered the office, his back to her, staring out through the somewhat grimy windows into the yard. His hands were tucked beneath his arms and Kate's gaze moved almost greedily over his broad shoulders. He was standing with his feet slightly apart, the powerful muscles of his thighs clearly outlined beneath the tight-fitting fabric of his trousers. Dear God, she thought, why did he arouse such a feeling of unwanted excitement in her? He wasn't the first man who'd come on to her since Sean died, and it was pathetic that this man, of all the men she'd known, had the ability to turn her bones to water.

'Sit down,' he said now, without turning. 'I expect you're wondering what this is all about.'

'Well, yes.' *No!* She thought she knew exactly what he was going to say. She just wished he'd get on with it instead of dragging it out.

He expelled a breath. 'Well, first of all, I suppose I should apologise for the way I behaved last week.' He paused. 'I've got no excuse. What I did was unforgivable. I invited you into my house and then abused your confidence in the most despicable way.'

Kate hadn't intended to sit down, but now she sank weakly into the chair at her side of the desk. She'd never imagined that he might be going to apologise, and the realisation of how quick she'd been to misjudge him filled her with remorse.

'Really, I—' she began awkwardly, but he wasn't finished.

'You probably think that's why I didn't come into the office for the rest of the week,' he continued, turning to face her, and although she was loath to meet his eyes her glancing look took in the stark contours of his face. 'Perhaps it was,' he added, his arms falling to his sides, his fingers finding diversion in the papers on the desk. 'Perhaps I was reluctant to admit the baseness of my actions even to myself. And it was easier to go away and put off this confrontation.'

'Mr Kellerman, please—'

'In my own defence, I have to say that I had good reasons for going to Doncaster. It's the last flat-racing classic of the year.' His lips twisted. 'I could also make the excuse that you—provoked me. It isn't very flattering to hear that your staff think you've got no guts.'

'I never said that—'

'Whatever.' Once again, he interrupted her. 'I've got only myself to blame for the opinion you must have of me now. I was half prepared to hear you'd given in your notice. You've probably got a case for sexual harassment, if you chose to take it that far.'

'I don't think so.' Kate shook her head rather bemusedly. She hesitated for a moment, and then went on, 'I'd rather forget it, if you don't mind.'

'So it didn't persuade you that I must be guilty of all the crimes I've been accused of?'

'No.'

'That's a relief.' His small smile was ironic. 'You must be the only woman in King's Montford who'd react that way.'

Kate lifted her shoulders. 'If—if you want me to leave—'

'I don't.'

His response was vehement, and she felt confident enough to stand again. 'Then I'll go and get on,' she said, moving round the chair and heading towards the door.

'Wait.' His hastily uttered summons arrested her, and she turned somewhat reluctantly to face him.

'Yes?'

'I've got a favour to ask,' he muttered, raking an impatient hand through his hair. 'I contacted my solicitor over the weekend, and he's arranged for me to have Rachel for the day.' He sucked in his breath. 'As I've only seen her a couple of times in the last two years, I want you to come with me to get her. Then, if her grandfather tries to pull any more stunts to stop me, it won't just be my word against his if he denies it later on.'

CHAPTER EIGHT

WYVERN HALL was an impressive sight. Its crenellated facade was more Victorian than Georgian, despite the fact that Alex had told her that parts of it dated back to the early nineteenth century. Nevertheless, Kate thought it was ugly, though that might have been because she was so apprehensive at being there.

She hadn't wanted to come. When he'd first made his request, she'd sought desperately for some means to avoid accompanying him to his father-in-law's house. Even though she knew that a good investigator would welcome any chance to learn more about her subject, she was reluctant. She was always afraid that someone might recognise her, for one thing, and for another, did she really want to get to know his daughter?

But her prime reason for wanting to refuse was a more personal one. She was already far too involved with Alex Kellerman, and getting caught up in his private affairs was the very last thing she should be doing. She was supposed to be *im*partial, *un*biased, not taking sides with him against a possibly innocent man. Conrad Wyatt only wanted to do what was right by his dead daughter. In his position, would she have behaved any differently?

'Pam's father wanted me to change my name to Wyatt,' Alex commented now as they reached the gravelled forecourt, and Kate acknowledged that all the misgivings in the world weren't going to do her any good. She was here; she'd agreed to do this favour; she was committed. She had to make the best of it for Rachel's sake, if nothing else.

'And you didn't want to do it,' she murmured now, and he gave her a sidelong look.

'No,' he said flatly. 'I prefer to bear my own name. But it wouldn't surprise me to learn that Conrad's trying to change Rachel's name to Wyatt, too.'

He was very bitter, thought Kate as he brought the Range Rover to a halt before the impressive entrance. But perhaps he had good reason. How would she have felt if Sean's parents had tried to take Joanne away from her? It hadn't happened, of course. Sean had never known his father, and his mother had died when he was just a teenager. Which perhaps explained why Kate's husband had had so little respect for his own marriage.

Kate wondered if Alex would expect her to stay in the car while he went and collected his daughter, but after pushing open his own door and getting out he came round the bonnet to open hers. He'd put on a long dark overcoat over his jacket, and she couldn't help noticing how well it suited him. But he'd left it unfastened so that when she passed him she smelt the clean male scent of his skin.

'Ready?' he asked, and she bit her lips to stop them from trembling.

'As I'll ever be,' she conceded, with more confidence in her words than in her voice.

'Good,' he said, and to her dismay he put a possessive hand beneath her elbow. 'Come on. You can take your cue from me.'

Which meant what? Kate looked up at him, aghast, but his attention was already concentrated on the house. His lean, dark features were harsh, and unforgiving, and she was very much afraid that Rachel would think so, too.

'Can I say something?' she asked in a low voice as he rang the doorbell, and she could tell by the way he turned to her that he half resented the distraction. But he nodded, albeit with some impatience, and she took a chance that he wouldn't bawl her out here. 'Lighten up,' she said. 'You don't want to frighten your daughter, do you?'

Alex blew out a breath. 'You don't know what——' he was

beginning harshly, when the door opened to reveal a young woman in a maid's uniform, and he bit off the words.

The maid regarded the visitors unsmilingly. 'Yes?' she said insolently, and Kate waited apprehensively for Alex to put the girl in her place.

But to her astonishment he didn't, and she watched the change come over his face. 'Will you tell Rachel's nanny that her father's come to collect her?' he asked, with a polite smile. 'She is expecting me.'

Kate breathed out slowly, hardly aware she had been holding the air in her lungs until the maid flounced away. 'Didn't I do well?' Alex asked softly, and she was amazed to see that he was still smiling. 'Oh, and thanks for the advice. I do tend to let the Wyatts rattle my cage.'

Kate smiled back, aware that her attraction to this man was as strong as ever. What was wrong with her? she wondered. She ought to have cut her losses last week and run. Now that Joanne had been suspended from school, she was unlikely to be allowed to go on the skiing trip, which had previously provided a justification for being here.

The maid was coming back accompanied by a middle-aged woman dressed in a beige sweater and a brown pleated skirt. 'The nanny,' said Alex in an undertone, but there was no sign of the little girl. Kate practically felt him stiffening beside her, and she prayed he wouldn't blow it now.

'I'm afraid Rachel and her grandfather are still down at the paddock,' said the nanny politely, and to Kate's relief there was no trace of animosity in her tone. 'I don't think Mr Wyatt expected you so early. If you'll come in, I'll have someone go and tell him you're here.'

'We'll go and meet them,' declared Alex at once, his relief evident. And, before the nanny could voice any objections, he anchored Kate with a hand at her wrist, and strode away.

They went around to the back of the house, where the Wyatts' stables adjoined a walled garden. It was not a professional operation like Alex's, but one or two horses nodded over the gates of the stalls. Apparently unaware that he was

still gripping her wrist, Alex led the way down a path between the garden and a barn. As they reached the end of the
path, Kate could see the paddock the nanny had mentioned,
and a little girl, riding a sorrel pony, being led around the
grassy enclosure by an elderly man with a deerstalker pulled
down over his ears.

Alex's hand tightened around her wrist for a moment and
then, as if realising he might be hurting her, he let her go.
And, in the same instant, the little girl noticed them, and her
excited cries of, 'Daddy, Daddy,' caused the elderly man to
turn his head in their direction.

The look Conrad Wyatt bestowed on his son-in-law was
full of malevolence, and Kate, who had tended to regard the
explanation Alex had given her as an exaggeration until now,
shivered. There was so much resentment in the old man's
gaze and a hatred that bordered on violence. She could believe anything of him, she realised incredulously, and she
looked at Alex to see how he would react.

But, to her relief, the younger man wasn't even looking at
his father-in-law. His attention was focussed on his daughter,
and, ignoring her grandfather's warning, Rachel swung her
leg across the saddle and, releasing her foot from the stirrup,
slid excitedly to the ground. Then, tossing her helmet on the
grass, she ran towards the white railings, and Alex leant
across the barrier and plucked her into his arms.

'Hello, sweetheart.'

His voice was gentler than Kate had ever heard it, and the
little girl wrapped her arms about his neck. 'I thought you
were never coming!' she exclaimed, pressing her pink cheek
against his neck. 'Grandpa said you'd prob'ly forgotten. Like
you did last week.'

Kate saw Alex's expression darken. 'Last week?' he echoed ominously as the old man handed the reins of the pony
to a waiting groom and came towards them, and Kate wanted
to grasp his arm and warn him not to say anything aggressive.

'Yes. Last week,' Conrad Wyatt repeated maliciously.

'Last Tuesday, as a matter of fact. Weren't you supposed to be coming to take Rachel out for the day?'

'He couldn't come,' broke in Kate, before Alex could answer him. Rachel had lifted her head from her father's shoulder and was looking at her now, and Kate gave her a big smile. 'Didn't your grandpa tell you?' she continued, much to the amazement of both men. 'Daddy phoned to say he was really sorry but he couldn't make it. It was my fault. I'm afraid I'd made an absolute mess of some work I was doing, and your daddy had to help me out.'

'Who are you?' asked Rachel, staring at her suspiciously, and her grandfather made a sound something like a hiss.

'Yes, who are you?' he snapped. 'And what do you know about it?' He sneered. 'Oh, yes. I suppose you're another of Kellerman's women.'

'She's my personal assistant,' put in Alex coolly, and Kate could tell from his expression that he understood exactly what she was trying to do. He looked at the little girl. 'I want you to meet Kate,' he said, gesturing her towards him. 'Kate, this is Rachel.' He cast a disparaging glance in his father-in-law's direction. 'My daughter.'

'Hello, Rachel.' Kate bestowed another warm smile on the little girl. She was a pretty little thing, though slightly underweight for her age, Kate decided, her seal-dark hair the image of her father's.

'Do you live at my daddy's house?' the child asked curiously, and before Kate could reply her grandfather gave another contemptuous snort.

'Of course she does, baby, just like all the others. Your father always had more time for his—'

'Are you coming to see your daddy's horses?' broke in Kate, before Conrad Wyatt could provoke Alex into violence. 'You're ever so lucky that your daddy has a farm. I wish mine did.'

'Rachel lives here, Miss Whoever-you-are,' ground out the old man angrily. 'And I'll thank you not to interrupt when I'm talking to my son-in-law.'

'I thought you were talking to Rachel,' remarked Alex calmly, and Kate realised he had no intention of playing the old man's game. He swung his daughter up onto his shoulders and she screamed excitedly. 'Now, if you don't mind, we're wasting far too much time. Say goodbye to your grandfather, sweetheart,' he added, and with Kate at his side he started back along the path.

'Bye, Grandpa,' Rachel shouted back over her shoulder. Then, clinging to her father's neck, she settled down to enjoy the ride.

'Don't forget to have her back for five o'clock,' Conrad Wyatt called after them. 'Any later than that and I'll be in touch with the police, Kellerman.'

'You do that,' muttered Alex, his long strides quickly opening up a space between them. Kate guessed there were other words he'd have liked to use to describe his feelings, but to her relief he kept them to himself.

'Where are we going?' demanded Rachel, after her father had settled her into the back of the Range Rover and secured her seat belt. She hesitated for just a moment. 'Jamaica Hill?'

'Eventually,' agreed Alex, folding his length behind the wheel. 'As it's a fine morning, I thought you might like to go and feed the ducks first. Then Kate and I can have a coffee at the snack bar, and you can have a chocolate milk shake.'

'Oooh, can I?'

This was evidently a treat and Kate found herself smiling as she looked out of the car window. But she would not be sorry to leave Wyvern Hall behind. Its grim façade seemed to reflect the personality of the people who lived there, and as she looked up at the windows she saw a pale face sheltering behind the glass.

Rachel's grandmother?

Kate frowned. The face was too quickly withdrawn to be seen clearly. All she got was an impression of vague hostility, and as there was no one else likely to look at her in that way she decided it must be Alex's mother-in-law. Naturally, she wouldn't approve of him bringing a woman with him, how-

ever innocent their relationship might be, and she was glad
when Alex spoke again and distracted her attention. She
didn't like the feeling that shadowy face had left her with.

'You don't mind, do you?'

Kate forced herself to remember what Alex had suggested,
but his words were barely audible over the roar as he gunned
the engine of the car. Still they reminded her that she'd only
agreed to come with him to pick up his daughter. Glancing
at Rachel again, she thought how long it seemed since she
and her daughter had done anything together. Was that why
Joanne had turned to shoplifting? To gain her mother's attention?

'Do you mind?'

Alex was speaking to her again, and she blinked away her
emotion. 'You're the boss,' she murmured, and his lips took
on an ironic curl.

'I wish I could believe that,' he remarked, and she wondered rather curiously what he meant.

Still, despite its rather shaky beginning, it was a good
morning. For a while, Kate managed to put her own problems
aside and concentrate on putting the little girl at her ease. It
didn't take her long to realise that although she reacted like
an ordinary four-year-old Rachel was by no means as confident as she appeared. Was that Alex's fault, Kate wondered,
or Conrad Wyatt's? She suspected it was a combination of
the two.

But Alex was trying his best to be a good father now, she
acknowledged. And there was no doubt that Rachel idolised
her father and hung on his every word. Without Conrad
Wyatt's interference these two could have worked things out,
she was sure of it. And, while it was true to say that the
child's grandfather had been there when she needed him, he
should have agreed to back off long ago.

Unfortunately, Conrad Wyatt wasn't the 'backing off'
type. Kate had realised that within a couple of minutes of
meeting the old man. If she hadn't been there, she wondered
if Alex would have let him get away with telling lies about

his absence. She doubted it. Which was probably how the Wyatts had retained control of Rachel for so long.

Alex was his own worst enemy, she realised. But, for all that, she could understand why he'd behaved as he had when Pamela was killed, so why couldn't his in-laws? The truth was, they probably could have, if they'd chosen to do so. But their daughter was dead, and Alex had played right into their hands.

Sitting in the snack bar later, watching Rachel making a valiant attempt to look as if she was enjoying the milk shake, Kate tried to understand Alex's feelings. She guessed he was worried about the child, and she could see why. Rachel was so delicate; so fragile; she looked as if the least thing would cause her to shatter. Her eyes, green, like her father's, were huge in the small oval of her face.

'Does he often tell Rachel lies about you?' Kate asked softly, cradling her coffee mug between her hands.

'How should I know?' Alex's tone was grim. 'I'm only her father.' He forced a smile to reassure the little girl, and then shrugged his shoulders wearily. 'It's all my fault. I should never have gone to pieces as I did.'

'Oh, I think that was justifiable,' murmured Kate, encouraging Rachel to taste one of the warm muffins her father had brought to tempt her. 'Mmm,' she said dramatically, breaking off a piece and eating it herself. 'That's scrummy. Can I have some more?'

'You can have it all,' said Rachel indifferently, pushing the plate away when Kate tried to persuade her. 'I don't have to eat anything I don't want to. My grandpa said.'

Alex expelled a controlled breath. 'He's got a lot to answer for,' he muttered. And then, forcing himself to taste the muffin, he endorsed Kate's opinion to the little girl. 'Sometimes we have to do things we don't want to do,' he told her gently. 'If you don't eat anything, you're never going to get as fat as me.'

'You're not fat!' exclaimed Rachel at once, her face dimpling, and while she was giggling her father popped a small piece of muffin into her mouth.

'I tell you what,' he said as she chewed experimentally. 'Let's see who can eat the most, shall we? And if you don't want Daddy to blow up like a balloon you'll have to make a proper effort.'

'All right.' Rachel sounded as if she might accept the challenge, but after swallowing only a couple of mouthfuls she pushed the plate away again. 'I'm not hungry,' she said. 'I want to go to your house. You said you were going to show me the new baby horse.'

'It's not a baby horse, it's a foal,' Alex corrected her, but he accepted defeat gracefully and got to his feet. 'Okay,' he said. 'Let's get this show on the road. And Jamaica Hill's not just my house, it's yours, too.'

'I don't want to live at Jamaica Hill,' said Rachel as they drove out of the park onto the Bath Road, and Alex exchanged a look with Kate that was full of pain.

'Why not?' he asked. 'It's your home. You've only been staying with Grandpa and Grandma because Daddy's been sick.'

'Have I?' Rachel sounded surprised at this explanation. 'Grandpa said you didn't want me to live with you any more.'

Alex clenched his teeth. 'That's not true,' he said harshly, and then, softening his tone, he added, 'I've missed you a lot. Jamaica Hill's not the same without my little girl.'

Kate glanced around and saw that Rachel was looking puzzled. 'It's true,' she said. 'Your daddy's really lonely in that big old house on his own.'

Rachel pursed her lips. 'But Grandpa said that now that Mummy's gone I'd be just an-noosuns. He said you'd prob'ly give my room to another little girl.'

'God!'

Alex swore violently, and Kate hurried to distract his daughter from her father's grief. 'You couldn't be more wrong,' she said. 'There are no other little girls at Jamaica

Hill.' She glanced at Alex. 'I'm sure Daddy told me your teddy was asking when you were going to come and see him again.'

Rachel's lips parted. 'Which teddy?'

'All of them,' put in her father, with a grateful look at Kate. 'So—does that mean you'd really like to come back and live with Daddy? Kate's right. I have been lonely since you went away.'

Rachel smiled. 'I want to live at Jamaica Hill,' she declared, nodding, and Kate saw Alex's hands tighten on the wheel.

'You will,' he said. 'Just as soon as I can arrange it.' He blew out a breath. 'Let's pretend you really do live there today, shall we?'

They were turning in to the gates of the estate when Rachel spoke again. 'Do you wish you had a little girl, Kate?' she asked thoughtfully, and Kate wondered what she was thinking. Was it just a casual question or did it mirror something else her grandfather had said?

'I have a little girl—well, quite a big girl really,' Kate replied, glancing at Alex. 'She lives with me in King's Montford, and her name's Joanne.'

'Joanne?'

'That's right.'

Rachel considered. 'Does she go to school?'

'Well, she does.' Kate pulled a wry face. 'But she's—on holiday at the moment.'

'Can I see her?'

'May I see her?' corrected her father automatically. And then he said, 'I don't see why not.' He raised his eyebrows at Kate. 'Why don't you bring her down to the yard one day?'

'To the stables?' Kate stared at him.

'Why not?' His lips twitched. 'She's got nothing else to do, has she?'

'That's not the point—'

'What is the point, then?' Alex frowned. 'Oh, I see. She's in the doghouse right now.'

And then his features relaxed into a grin when Rachel asked, 'What's a doghouse?'

'Joanne was—naughty,' Kate explained, unhappily aware that she and Alex were becoming far too familiar. But that was what happened when you allowed a relationship to encroach on your private life, she reflected. He already knew more about her than was strictly sensible. And it wasn't just unwise, it was downright dangerous to let it go on.

'How was she naughty?' asked Rachel, and Kate was thinking so hard about how to answer her that she didn't notice that Alex had driven up to the house. She'd been expecting him to drop her at the stables, but now he was turning off the engine and Mrs Muir was at the door of the house, waiting to greet them.

She turned to him then, her eyes wide with enquiry, and he gave her a rueful look. 'Humour me,' he pleaded softly. 'I want to make up to you for what happened last week.'

'But, Rachel—'

'Rachel won't mind.' He glanced round at his daughter who was busily removing her seat belt. 'You don't mind if Kate has lunch with us, do you?'

'Will Joanne be having lunch, too?' Rachel asked at once, scrambling forward, and Alex exchanged another amused look with Kate.

'Not today,' he said at last. 'But maybe next time you come to visit. Look, there's Mrs Muir. You'll have to make do with her for today.'

Rachel looked as if she might protest, but then she saw the fluffy toy Mrs Muir was carrying and Joanne was forgotten. 'Peter!' she exclaimed. 'It's Peter Rabbit.' And as soon as the door was opened for her she jumped out, wrapping her arms around the cuddly bunny, and beaming all over her face.

Kate got out rather more sedately. She wasn't at all convinced that she was doing the right thing. In fact she was fairly sure she was doing the wrong one, and even the warmth of Mrs Muir's welcome didn't help to put her at her ease.

Still, there wasn't a lot she could do about it now. Everyone seemed to be taking it for granted that she was staying, and it would have been churlish to refuse. Besides, much as she feared their developing relationship, it could prove useful, and she squashed her initial prejudice beneath a veneer of polite forbearance.

All the same, that forbearance quickly wore thin when Mrs Muir took Rachel off to the kitchen with her, leaving Kate and Alex in the library. Once again, they were alone together, and Kate had the added distraction of knowing that she was nowhere near as indifferent to him as she'd have him believe.

'Drink?' he offered, as before, and this time Kate decided she needed something slightly stronger than orange juice to sustain her.

'Um—do you have a martini?' she asked, linking her cold fingers together, and Alex bent to open the cabinet door.

'I think so,' he said, dropping ice cubes into a tall glass. Then, looking up, he said, 'Make yourself at home.'

As if she could!

Kate managed a tight smile nevertheless, and subsided into the armchair she'd occupied the last time she was here. Holding her hands towards the fire, she tried to force herself to relax, but her knees persisted in trembling and she pressed them together to hide her nervousness.

'There you go.'

She hadn't heard Alex cross the room. The richly patterned carpet had silenced his footsteps, but now he was beside her, the drink she had requested extended towards her.

'Oh—oh, thanks.' Her face burned suddenly, and she heard him mutter something under his breath.

'It's okay.' His voice when he spoke revealed his frustration. Then, going back to the cabinet, he helped himself to a beer from the fridge before continuing, 'You can trust me, you know. I don't usually try to seduce my guests.' His lips twisted. 'Well, not on a first date anyway.'

'It wasn't a date.'

'No.' He acknowledged her correction. 'Which makes it worse, doesn't it? I took advantage of you without even paying the bill.'

Kate pressed her lips together. 'Let's forget about it, shall we?' She sipped her martini. 'This is nice.'

'Not too strong for you?' he asked mockingly. 'I wouldn't want to be accused of trying to get you drunk.'

Kate sighed and looked up at him. 'Would you like me to go? I can, you know. You can always tell Mrs Muir that Joanne is ill or something.'

'Why would I want to do that?' Alex sighed, too, his impatience evident. 'No, I just want us to stop sniping at each other. I'd like you to stay.' He paused, and then added softly, 'I hope we can be friends.'

Friends?

Kate almost choked on her drink. Dear God, if he ever found out who she was he'd be—uncontrollable. She had been thinking 'furious', but that wasn't a strong enough adjective to describe how he'd feel. Her breath caught in her throat. He'd never forgive her; never. She'd have to spend the rest of her life looking over her shoulder, afraid of every shadow after dark.

'Look,' she began awkwardly, 'you don't have to say anything. There's nothing either of us can do to change the past, and I'd rather pretend it never happened.' She waited a beat, and then, with a complete change of subject, asked, 'Are—are you and Mrs Sheridan good friends?'

'Lacey?' His eyes narrowed. 'I guess so. Why do you ask?'

Kate shrugged. 'Um, Ted—Ted Lowes, that is—said she'd gone to Doncaster with you.'

'Ah.'

He sounded resigned, and she hoped she hadn't said anything she shouldn't. The last thing she wanted to do was make him think she'd been gossiping about him. Or that Ted had been gossiping either. Especially since the head groom had proved depressingly reticent about his boss.

'That was Mrs Sheridan who—who—'

'Interrupted us last week?' suggested Alex dryly, and she hoped he'd been diverted by her words. 'Yes, that was Lacey,' he agreed, and then grimaced. 'She and I have known one another a long time.'

'Really?'

Kate tried not to sound too interested, and, as she'd hoped, he continued in a similar vein. 'Her land adjoins Jamaica Hill on the western boundary. When my father was alive, he and her husband were good friends.'

'But he doesn't accompany her to race meetings?'

Kate couldn't hide her curiosity and Alex regarded her sardonically. 'She's a widow,' he amended. 'Her husband was much older than she was and he died a few years ago. Since then...' he paused '...since then, she and I have attempted to sustain the connection. Unfortunately, it hasn't always worked.'

'No?'

'No.' Once again Kate's comment had prompted a reaction. 'She never did forgive me for marrying Pam.' He mused. 'And when Alicia was here she didn't like that either. She couldn't wait to get her out of the house.'

'Alicia?' Kate managed to sound as if the name was not familiar to her.

'Yeah, Alicia Sawyer,' he conceded, but she sensed she'd spoken out of turn. 'She worked at the stables before you came,' he added, almost as an afterthought. He nodded towards the glass in her hand. 'Would you like another?'

'What?' Kate had been so intent on what he was saying that she hardly heard the question. 'Oh—oh, no,' she mumbled, when her brain kicked into action again. 'Um—' She hesitated. 'This is fine, thank you.' And then, after another pregnant pause, she asked, 'Did she find another job?'

'Who?'

Now it was his turn to be obtuse, and she had to force herself to continue. 'Al—Alicia,' she murmured, pretending an innocence she didn't feel.

'She left,' he responded shortly. 'Rather suddenly.' His face hardened. 'I prefer not to discuss Mrs Sawyer, if you don't mind.'

'I'm sorry.'

Of course, Kate did mind, but she could hardly tell him that. And at least he wasn't afraid to discuss her departure, which must say something about his state of mind.

'It doesn't matter,' he declared indifferently now. 'I guess I'm touchy where Mrs Sawyer is concerned.' He paused. 'But Lacey means well,' he added, reverting to his earlier topic. 'I'm not always the most tolerant of men.'

Kate saw the opening and took it. 'Does Mrs Sheridan breed horses, too?'

'She owns a couple of mares and a prize stallion, but I wouldn't call her a breeder,' replied Alex flatly. 'She doesn't have the facilities for breeding. She prefers someone else to deal with that side of things.'

'You?' asked Kate guilelessly, and then coloured at the possible connotation. 'I mean, you do breed horses, don't you? You have such a lot.'

'I actually own very few horses,' Alex told her tolerantly. 'But, yes, I have the facilities for breeding here at Jamaica Hill, as you say.'

'But—'

Kate was confused now, and he went on to enlighten her. 'My business is mainly concerned with boarding other people's horses,' he explained levelly. 'We can arrange for a mare to be covered—serviced—if that's what the owner wants, but most of our work is involved in exercising and training young animals, as I'm sure you'll have gathered by now.'

'But you go to race meetings.'

'I go to horse sales, too, both here and in the United States, but I'm usually acting on behalf of someone else.'

Kate shook her head. 'I thought—' she began, before breaking off, and he uttered a short laugh.

'What? That I owned all the horseflesh in my stables?' he asked drolly. 'I'm not a rich man, Kate, whatever impression you may have gained from the tabloids when Pam died.'

Kate was embarrassed. 'I didn't mean to imply—' She made a helpless gesture. 'Tell me about how you started. Have you always wanted to work with horses?'

'Actually, I wanted to be a psychologist,' he admitted ruefully. 'But my father wasn't having any of that. I was his only offspring, you see, and he was determined I'd take over this place when he retired.'

Kate nodded. 'But you didn't mind?'

'I minded like hell, but it didn't do me any good,' Alex replied, pulling a wry face. 'But I like to think I've put some of that instinctive training to good use.'

Kate was interested. 'How?'

'Well, they say that to train a horse you've got to use psychology. You concentrate on three things: its physical abilities, its skill, and its mental fitness. A lot depends on a horse's temperament. You can have the fittest animal in the world, but if its nature is inherently bad there's not a lot you can do with it.'

'But how do you know? I mean—' Kate tried to clarify what she meant '—how do you know when a horse is—say, bad-tempered?'

Alex was silent for so long, she thought he wasn't going to answer her. But then he said, 'Vicious horses tend to lay their ears back and bare their teeth.' He paused. 'If you're trying to find out why my wife would choose to mount a horse like that, why don't you come right out and say so? It's not as if I haven't been asked that question before.'

'I'm not.' Kate was ashamed to admit that nothing had been further from her thoughts.

He scowled. 'Well, the truth is, Jackson—that was the name of the horse she was riding when she had the accident—didn't always exhibit his psychosis. He was only uncontrollable at times, but I'd already decided to get rid of him.'

Kate hesitated. 'I suppose you wish you had now.'

'Yeah, right.' Alex was predictably bitter. 'Then I might have been dumb enough to be bringing up two children that weren't my own.'

Kate gasped. 'Rachel's yours!' she exclaimed. 'I don't know how you can doubt it. Her hair, her eyes, her mouth—' She caught herself before she incriminated herself further. 'I—I'm sure you don't need to have any worries on—on that score.'

Alex's expression had softened. 'I'm glad to hear it.' His eyes played about her mouth. 'And I suppose I should be flattered that you seem so well-informed.'

Kate buried her nose in her drink, conscious that the atmosphere between them was subtly changing again. It seemed she couldn't be alone with this man without becoming aware of him in a totally personal way.

Rachel's return a few moments later, to announce that lunch was ready, provided a welcome escape from her dilemma. Instead of watching her, Alex was obliged to watch his daughter, and she kept him busy with a host of questions of her own. They ranged from when she was going to be allowed to spend the night at Jamaica Hill with him to the new foal he intended to show her that afternoon. When they went in to lunch, Kate noticed that the little girl only picked at her meal again, but what she lacked in appetite she definitely made up for in charm.

After the meal, she insisted on showing Kate her bedroom. She was obviously reassured to find it looked exactly the same as it had done the last time she was here. Kate guessed Alex kept it that way deliberately. The toys, the paper on the walls, even the soft furnishings, were all to suit a much younger child than Rachel was now.

Once back at the stables, Kate excused herself and went into her office. Much as she would have liked to stay with Alex and his daughter, she knew she had to remember why she was here. The trouble was, the longer she knew Alex, the more she became convinced that he was innocent. Which wasn't at all the purpose behind why Henry Sawyer had persuaded her to take this job...

CHAPTER NINE

'SO WHAT have you found out?'

Henry Sawyer faced Kate across the desk in her office at the agency, a scowl of impatience darkening his already sullen features. He'd rung Susie the day before to arrange this meeting, once again after normal working hours, which Kate thought was just as well.

She could hardly have asked for any more time off, she reflected ruefully, fidgeting with her pen. What excuse could she have given Alex? That she was meeting with the man who was trying to ruin his life?

She knew Sawyer expected her to have some information for him, but the fact was, she needed more time. It wasn't possible to gain a person's confidence in the space of a few short weeks, particularly when the press had already given Alex such a raw deal. And everyone who worked at Jamaica Hill was sensitive to any questions of a personal nature.

'I know that your wife worked for Mr Kellerman until about eleven weeks ago,' she said now, and Henry Sawyer gave a derisive snort.

'I know that. I told you!' he exclaimed scornfully. 'I mean—do you know where she is? Has Kellerman dropped any clues?'

As if he would!

'He—he did say she left quite suddenly,' she admitted at last, chiding herself for the sense of guilt she felt at revealing this much to him.

'I'll bet he did,' muttered the man opposite. 'If she ever left at all. That bastard's got all the answers. You want to watch yourself, Mrs Ross. You're not unlike Alicia yourself.'

Kate caught her breath. 'That's nonsense,' she protested at

once, pretending to be checking some detail in the file to avoid meeting his accusing gaze. But she couldn't disguise her burning cheeks, and she prayed he'd think it was embarrassment and nothing else.

'No.' Sawyer leaned towards her confidingly. 'You're a good-looking woman, Mrs Ross. He likes them slim and blonde, though it's a pity you don't have more up top, if you know what I mean.'

Kate didn't know whether to be flattered or offended but she chose the latter. 'We're not here to talk about me, Mr Sawyer,' she said tersely. 'And—and as far as your wife is concerned I'm fairly sure she left of her own free will.'

'So where is she?'

He was belligerent now, and Kate expelled a weary sigh. 'I don't know,' she conceded honestly. 'I am making some progress, but it's a slow business, I'm afraid.'

'You call telling me what I already know "some progress"?' he snapped irritably, and Kate wished she could wash her hands of the whole affair.

'It takes time to gain people's confidence,' she said. 'I don't want to draw attention to myself. If I start asking a lot of awkward questions, Mr Kellerman will become—suspicious. If he does and throws me out, I'll have wasted my time and your money.'

'My money? Oh, yeah.' Henry Sawyer chewed on his lower lip. 'It wouldn't do to waste that, would it?' His eyes narrowed. 'I might just decide I want it back.'

'Not a chance.' Kate was angry now. How dared he sit there patronising her, and behaving as if he was doing her a favour by calling in? 'My time is money, Mr Sawyer. I explained that before I agreed to take the case. And by my reckoning, your payments are now in arrears. Now, if you don't like what I'm doing, I'll give you an invoice showing what's been spent and then you can settle the balance.'

'That won't be necessary.' His voice was sulky now, and she breathed a little easier knowing she had had her say. 'But, well, Mr—that is, me—*I'm* getting really worried,' he mut-

tered disjointedly. 'In another week or so it'll be three months
since she disappeared.'

Kate wished she felt like sympathising with him, but the
more she saw of Henry Sawyer, the more convinced she became that Alicia had left of her own accord. She couldn't
imagine what the woman had ever seen in him, unless it was
Alicia's disappearance that had caused him to lose interest in
himself.

Having given her another substantial sum of money, he
left soon afterwards with Kate's promise that she'd be in
touch if she had any news. She had his address, though no
phone number, she noticed. Evidently Mr Sawyer preferred
to do business face to face.

She got home about half-past seven to find a note from
her mother propped beside the kettle. It appeared that Ellen
Ross had taken Joanne to the cinema in Bath and they
wouldn't be back until fairly late. Kate remembered now that
Joanne had mentioned the film she wanted to see and her
grandmother must have decided to treat her. Kate guessed
her daughter would welcome any chance to get out of the
house.

Which reminded her of what Alex Kellerman had said
about bringing Joanne down to the stables. But it had been
mooted when she had had lunch with him and his daughter
and it hadn't been mentioned since. Of course, she hadn't
seen much of him since Sam Guthrie's return to work. Had
he meant it, or was it just something he'd said in passing?
After all, it had been Rachel who'd expressed a desire to
meet her.

But there was no denying that Joanne would have loved
the chance to visit the stables. She'd never had much to do
with horses, but she loved all animals and it was only because
of the local council's regulations that she didn't have a pet
at the flat. Still, it probably wasn't the most sensible thing to
do in the circumstances. She was already regretting her involvement with Alex Kellerman. It would be most unwise to
involve her daughter as well.

Ellen had left Kate's evening meal in the oven. It was giving off an appetising aroma of meat and onions, but when Kate lifted the casserole onto the hob it quickly lost its appeal. At least an hour stewing in its own juices had left the meal looking dark and rubbery, and a burnt skin of gravy clung to the edges of the dish.

Deciding she'd rather make herself an omelette later, Kate hung her coat in the closet and went into her bedroom. Turning on the lamp, she dropped her bag on the bed and viewed her reflection in the dressing-table mirror. She looked as dejected as she felt, she thought dully, pulling the elastic band from her braid and threading her fingers through her loosened hair. Was she really cut out to be an investigator? she wondered. Wouldn't she be happier if she was working at the stables for real?

She suspected the answer was yes, which meant that Henry Sawyer had some justification for his impatience. Was he right? Was Alex Kellerman really a dangerous man? One thing was certain and that was that her loyalties were becoming hopelessly divided. She was a fool. Any dimwit would know better than to get personally involved with a case.

Abandoning such depressing thoughts, she went into the bathroom. A soak in the tub was what she needed, she determined, turning on the taps. And then afterwards she might open a bottle of wine, she thought, peeling off her shirt and bra. She'd forget all about Alex Kellerman and Henry Sawyer. By the time her mother and Joanne got back, she'd be feeling pleasantly mellow.

She was drying herself when she heard someone ringing the doorbell. She'd taken the portable radio into the bathroom with her so she couldn't be sure how long the ringing had been going on. It couldn't be her mother and Joanne. Her mother would have used her key. Unless she'd lost it. Kate frowned, reaching for her velvet sweatpants. Either way, she was going to have to find out.

The loose-fitting shirt that matched the purple sweatpants clung to her damp body, but she couldn't help it. It was better than wrapping a towel about herself to go to the door. The pants clung to her legs, too, but at least her body was drying. Her hair was another matter, and she scooped it up into a knot on top of her head.

She half hoped the ringing would have stopped by the time she got there, but it hadn't, and she secured the safety chain before opening the door. It was just a precaution, and she doubted it would hold a determined assailant, but her mother felt safer with the sturdy chain in place.

However, her jaw sagged when she saw who had disturbed her. Alex Kellerman was standing in the corridor outside. 'Hello,' he said stiffly. 'I hope I'm not interrupting anything.'

Kate didn't know what to say; what to think even. She couldn't imagine why he might have come to see her, unless by some awful mistake on her part he'd found out who she was.

'I—no,' she said now, putting a nervous hand up to her damp hair. 'I—I was just getting out of the bath, that's all.' She licked her dry lips. 'Have you been waiting long?'

'Not long,' he replied, with a dismissing shrug of his shoulders. He was wearing a dark blue three-piece suit this evening and the more formal clothes added to his darkly sensual appeal. 'I saw your car downstairs, as it happens. I took the chance that you might be in.'

'Oh—yes.' Kate acknowledged the fact with a shiver of awareness. It reminded her of how vulnerable she was. Thank goodness he'd known where to find her. If he'd asked someone for directions, they might have mistaken him for a client. It was frightening to think she could have been found out.

'I expect you're wondering what I'm doing here,' he said now, and she realised she'd have to remove the safety chain. Despite her misgivings, she couldn't go on talking to him through the crack.

'You'd better come in,' she said, putting the chilliness she was feeling down to the draught that blew along the corridor. She unfastened the chain and opened the door. 'It's through there.'

'Thanks.'

Although she stepped aside, he still brushed her arm as he went past her into the living room of the flat. She wondered if he was as aware of it as she was. Probably not, she reflected wryly. For the past few days, he'd seemed more than willing to forget that he'd wanted them to be friends.

Because he hadn't meant it, she chided herself irritably, closing the door and following him along the hall. The last thing he'd have wanted was for there to be any unpleasantness between them while Rachel was visiting. He'd needed someone to go with him to fetch his daughter and she'd been available. Giving her lunch had been for Rachel's sake, not hers.

He was standing in the middle of the floor when she entered the lamplit living room, and Kate was immediately conscious of how ill-at-ease he looked. He didn't belong here, she thought. Despite his notoriety, he belonged in more elegant surroundings. In his expensive suit and hand-made shoes, he made the modest room look cheap.

'Do you want to sit down?' she asked offhandedly, gesturing towards the sofa. Then, smoothing her sweating palms over her rear, she said, 'Can I offer you a drink?'

'I don't want anything right now,' Alex said, but he subsided onto the edge of the sofa. He glanced about him with what Kate was sure was feigned interest. 'I've often wondered what your home was like.'

'So now you know.' Kate's bare feet curled into the rust-coloured carpet. 'It's nothing like Jamaica Hill, as you can see. But we like it.' She gripped the backs of her thighs self-consciously. 'Is something wrong? Is that why you're here?'

His eyes seemed mesmerised by her nervous probing. He'd been watching her hands, but now he dragged his gaze up to her face. There was a certain satisfaction to be gained from the fact that he had to look up at her. It was an advantage that she'd never had before.

'No,' he replied now, his low voice fairly scraping over her nerves. 'As a matter of fact, I came to see Joanne.'

'Joanne?' Kate couldn't hide her astonishment. 'Um—well, she's not here. She's gone to the movies with my mother.'

'A pity,' he said, seeming to see that as his cue to get to his feet again. 'Then I suppose there's no point in asking what time she'll be home?'

Kate shook her head. 'They've gone into Bath,' she murmured. 'I could give her a message.'

His green eyes darkened. 'Yeah, I guess you could,' he agreed. 'But I'd prefer to speak to her myself.'

Kate stepped back. 'All right,' she said. 'If it's something private.'

'It's not.' He took a breath. 'Perhaps I just wanted an excuse to come and see you again.'

'I don't think so.' Kate gave him a thin smile. 'You can see me any time. I'm still working at the stables, you know.'

'I know.'

His gaze was disturbingly intent and Kate wondered why he'd really come here. She didn't buy his story about speaking to Joanne. Yet he knew she lived here with her mother and daughter, so he could hardly have anticipated that she would be alone.

'Tell me,' he said, taking a deliberate step towards her, and Kate had to steel herself not to panic as she'd done in the library at Jamaica Hill, 'what do you really think of me? Do I scare you? Do you still have doubts about my innocence, about the way Pam died?'

Kate pulled a breath deep into her lungs before answering him. 'You don't scare me,' she insisted firmly, but that wasn't all he'd asked and she knew it.

'But you're not sure if I was to blame for Pamela's accident,' he stated flatly. His expression hardened. 'Well, at least I know where I stand.'

'I didn't mean—'

'Tell Joanne I'll be in touch with her in the next few days,' he said, stepping around her, and before she could gather her thoughts he'd reached the living-room door.

'No. Wait—' she began, knowing she couldn't let him go thinking the worst of her, and his shoulders slumped as he swung back against the jamb.

'What?' he demanded harshly. 'Oh, right. You don't want Joanne anywhere near me.'

'It's not that—'

'Then what is it? Some new excuse for not inviting her to Jamaica Hill?'

'No.' Kate sighed, and then, reluctantly, she closed the space between them. 'I—I do think you're innocent. I don't think you—deliberately—brought about your wife's death.'

Alex tipped his head back against the frame of the door behind him and looked at her through his lashes. 'Is that supposed to be an apology?' he asked. 'You don't think I *deliberately* put Jackson in that stall?' He gave a bitter laugh. 'But you do think I put the horse in there, don't you? Whether by accident, or simple misjudgement, I'm to blame?'

Kate's hair was starting to come loose from its band, and, pulling it off, she thrust her fingers into the damp mass of curls. 'I don't know what to think,' she admitted helplessly. 'I wasn't there. I don't know all the facts. But I don't believe you're guilty. Isn't that enough?'

Alex expelled a weary breath. 'I guess it's going to have to be.'

He sounded totally defeated, and Kate suppressed an almost irresistible urge to scream. She wanted to tell him she trusted him, that there was no way he could have hurt his wife, but the reason why she wanted to believe him was what really held her back.

He was turning towards the outer door when she spoke again. 'What—what you said,' she murmured. 'About—about inviting Joanne to the stables. Is that really why you came tonight?'

'What else?'

His response was muffled. Deliberately, she suspected. He was feeling in his pocket for his car keys and the words were

lost as he reached for the latch. Which was when Kate reacted, when she knew she couldn't let him go like this, and,
shouldering past him, she pressed her back against the door.

'Don't go.'

'Why not?' Alex's expression didn't alter. 'I'm sure you'd
rather I left before your mother and daughter get home.'

Kate hesitated for a moment and then surrendered to a
force stronger than herself. 'They won't be home for hours,'
she told him huskily. 'At least stay and have a drink.'

Alex stepped away from the door. 'I don't think that would
be entirely wise in the present circumstances,' he said tightly.

'Why not?' She threw his words back at him now. Then
she asked audaciously, 'Have you got something more important to do?'

His lips twisted. 'I think so.'

She couldn't stop herself. 'What?'

'Getting out of here,' he answered, without emotion.
'Now, do you want to get out of the way so that I can open
the door?'

'And if I don't?'

His lips parted to deliver what she was sure would have
been a passionate response, but then he seemed to gather
himself and when he spoke again his voice was low and
controlled. 'Let's stop playing games, shall we? We both
know what would happen if I accepted your invitation, and
I have no desire to be accused of harassing you again.'

Kate was indignant. 'I didn't accuse you of harassing me,'
she protested, and he gave her a weary look.

'No. Okay. You didn't accuse me of it, but you damn near
sprinted out of the library the last time I laid a hand on you.'

Kate bent her head. 'That woman came in.'

'Lacey; right.' He conceded the point. 'But you weren't
exactly—co-operating before that.'

'No.' Kate had to admit that was true.

'No.' He breathed deeply. 'Point taken, I think.'

Kate frowned. 'But—didn't you care?'

His eyes narrowed. 'Yeah. I cared like hell.'

'No.' She shook her head. 'I meant about—about Mrs Sheridan interrupting us.'

'Not particularly.'

'But you must have done.'

'Why?'

'Well—you're close friends.'

His nostrils flared. 'Kate, I've known Lacey for more than ten years, and if she chooses to walk into my house unannounced she can't complain if what she sees doesn't meet with her unqualified approval.'

'Do you think she'd have walked out again?'

He grimaced. 'Knowing Lacey, I doubt it.'

'There you are, then.'

'What? Are you saying her arrival gave you the excuse to go haring out of there as if the devil himself was at your heels? For God's sake, a stranger would have thought I'd been assaulting you!' Then he gave a cynical snort. 'Well, hell, I suppose I was.'

'You weren't.' Kate spoke impulsively, and then had to stand his disbelieving appraisal. 'It—it wasn't like that,' she muttered awkwardly. 'I—I provoked you, like you said. I had no right to criticise your way of dealing with—with your life.'

Alex's dark brows arched. 'And that gave me the right to take advantage of you?' he asked mockingly, and she sighed.

'You're making this very hard.'

'Perhaps that's my purpose in life.'

'What?'

'To make things hard for people.'

'To make things hard for yourself,' burst out Kate impatiently. 'I thought you wanted us to be friends.'

'I find I no longer have any inclination in that direction,' he told her harshly. 'And as far as making things hard for myself is concerned, believe me, you have no idea.'

Kate pushed herself away from the door. 'Then tell me,' she said imploringly. 'I do want to understand.'

'Do you?' His eyes moved to some place behind her head

and she could see the battle he was having with himself to resist her argument. 'I don't think you have any conception of how I feel.'

'Then tell me!' she exclaimed urgently, and with a groan of defeat he turned back towards the living room.

'I guess I will take you up on that offer of a drink,' he said flatly, and Kate felt a mixture of apprehension and relief.

This time, Alex didn't wait for her invitation to sit down. Unbuttoning his jacket again, he flung himself onto the sofa, and Kate gathered herself sufficiently to ask him what he'd like to drink.

'You don't have a great deal of choice,' she admitted rue-fully. 'Just wine, or beer, or a soft drink.' She hesitated. 'Have you eaten?'

Alex tilted his head to look up at her. 'Are you going to feed me, too?' he asked, with gentle mockery, and the warmth of his smile sent rivulets of heat into her quivering stomach.

'Well, I was going to make myself an omelette,' she ad-mitted. 'And maybe a salad.' She paused. 'If you'd like to join me, I'm sure there's enough for two.'

Alex studied her face for what seemed like eons, but which was probably just a few seconds, and then he nodded. 'Sounds good,' he conceded. 'If you don't mind?'

In fact, Kate was wondering what had possessed her to invite him for a meal. After tasting Mrs Muir's cooking, she was unhappily aware that her efforts just didn't compare, and eggs and salad were hardly appropriate fare.

'You wouldn't rather have pizza, would you?' she asked hurriedly. 'I can send out for—'

'An omelette is fine with me,' Alex told her firmly, and, getting to his feet again, he took off his jacket and slung it over the back of a chair. 'Come on. I'll help you.'

Kate led the way into the kitchen wishing she'd stuck at offering him a beer. The kitchen at the flat was small and obviously much different from the kitchen at Jamaica Hill, and she was overwhelmingly aware of his powerful bulk in the confined space.

'Did—did you decide what you wanted to drink?' she asked, determining not to let him see how he disturbed her, thrusting the cold casserole back into the cooker out of sight.

'I'll wait till we eat,' he said, propping his hips against the breakfast bar. He shrugged. 'What do you want me to do?'

'There's not a lot to do.' Kate took the bag of lettuce from the fridge and shook it into a dish. 'You could open the wine, I suppose.'

'Fine. Where is it?'

'It's in the fridge, too,' she replied, turning back for eggs and tomatoes. She handed the bottle to him and indicated a drawer. 'The corkscrew's in there.'

She noticed that he loosened the collar of his shirt and pulled his tie away before tackling the bottle. He'd already turned the sleeves of his shirt back to his elbows, and she was unwillingly fascinated by the light covering of hair that darkened his wrists. His watch was a plain gold one, she observed, on a tan-coloured leather strap.

'Did you know your husband was seeing another woman?' he asked abruptly, and she bit back an unwary exclamation.

'I beg your pardon?'

He fixed the corkscrew in place before giving her a side-long look. 'I think you heard me,' he said quietly. 'Did you?'

Kate caught her breath. 'Why do you want to know?'

'Humour me.'

She hesitated for a few moments, and then said tightly, 'No. No, I didn't.'

'Me, neither,' he remarked, attacking the cork. 'Know that Pam was having an affair, I mean.' He gave a derisive snort. 'I must have been the only one who didn't.'

Kate turned her head to look at him. 'What do you mean?'

He paused in what he was doing and blew out a breath. 'Because the man involved worked for me.'

Kate's lips parted. 'He was a groom?'

'No.' Alex sighed. 'He worked on the estate.' He considered for a moment, and then said flatly, 'His name was Muir. Philip Muir.'

Kate gasped. 'Mrs Muir's son?'

'You know about her son?' Alex frowned, and Kate hurried to explain.

'I know he died,' she said quickly. 'I—I met Mrs Muir in the supermarket last week, and she invited me to have tea with her in the café. She was asking me about Sean, and I told her he'd been killed in a car crash. That's when she told me that both her son and her husband were dead.'

The furrow between Alex's brows deepened. 'And did she tell you anything else?'

Guessing he meant had the housekeeper been gossiping, Kate shook her head. 'It was all perfectly innocent,' she assured him. 'Your name was hardly mentioned. She certainly didn't talk about your wife, if that's what you're getting at.'

Alex's shoulders sagged. 'No.' He gave a slight nod of his head. 'I should have known better than to ask something like that. So you won't know that Philip took his own life about six weeks before Pam was killed?'

Kate looked stunned. 'I had no idea. Was it—was it— connected?'

'With Pam being pregnant, you mean?' Alex pulled out the cork with undue force. 'You could say that, I suppose. She'd apparently finished with him a couple of weeks before it happened.'

'Oh, no.' Kate was appalled. Then she frowned. 'But I thought you said you hadn't known about the affair.'

Alex's expression grew sardonic. 'Still checking up on me, Mrs Hughes?' he mocked disarmingly. 'I didn't. The Muirs told me—after Pam was dead.'

Kate expelled an unsteady breath. 'I wasn't checking up on you,' she protested, but to herself she wondered if that was entirely true. Yet she doubted she would be reporting their conversation to Henry Sawyer. It was far too important to her to be sullied by his coarse claims.

'Whatever.' Alex turned to watch her now as she broke

half a dozen eggs into a bowl. Then, as she picked up the whisk and began to beat them, his eyes lowered to her bosom, and in a strangled voice he said, 'Are you wearing anything under that suit?'

The whisk clattered into the bowl and Kate's face turned scarlet. 'Do you always ask such personal questions?' she asked. 'Or do you just enjoy shocking me?'

'I was interested,' murmured Alex huskily. 'I was remembering how soft your skin was that afternoon in the library, and how much I wanted to take your clothes off.' His eyes grew sensual on hers. 'Of course, I wouldn't have done it. Take your clothes off, I mean. I wouldn't have wanted to embarrass Mrs Muir.'

Kate expelled a sound that mingled disbelief with outrage. 'But you don't have any qualms about embarrassing me!'

'Am I embarrassing you?' He had been lounging against the counter beside her, but now he came abruptly to his feet. 'I'm sorry. I guess I was just thinking out loud.'

'Do you think that makes me feel any better?' Kate groped for the whisk again but her hand was shaking so much that she couldn't go on beating the eggs.

'Do you want me to go?' he asked tensely, and she knew that even now she had only to say the word and he'd walk out of the apartment. She wondered how she could ever have doubted this man's innocence. If it wasn't such a crazy—futile—notion she'd have said she was falling in love with him herself.

'What do you think?' she demanded now, half snappily, her own emotions working overtime as she fought to bring them under control. She caught her breath. 'You should know better than that. Dammit, you know that's not what I want.'

'Do I?'

He looked down at her with eyes that seemed to burn with a latent fire, and she swayed towards him, half afraid he still doubted her even now. Her hands spread against his waistcoat, her thumbs catching on the buttons, feeling the strong beat of his heart throbbing in his chest.

She breathed a little sigh of relief when he bent his head towards her, and when his lips brushed hers she parted them to his tongue. His hand gripped the back of her neck, pulling her closer to him, and he deepened the kiss with the hungry pressure of his mouth.

His hands possessed her, moving over her shoulders with spine-tingling familiarity, creating an intimacy between them that she'd never known with any other man. His fingers explored the sensitive curve of her back as his tongue sought and stroked the quivering length of hers, drawing her lower lip into his mouth and biting gently on the vulnerable inner flesh.

Kate's knees almost buckled when his hands invaded the waistband of her sweatpants, cupping her bare bottom and bringing her fully against him.

'I knew you weren't wearing anything else,' he muttered huskily against the whorl of her ear, and she clutched his neck to prevent herself from sagging to the floor. 'Open your legs,' he added urgently, and although she was too bemused to consciously follow his direction he had no difficulty in inserting his muscled thigh between hers.

The touch of his leg pressing against that most sensitive part of her anatomy was breathtaking, the rub of the soft cloth of the sweatpants causing a damp heat that she was sure he must be able to feel. She felt as if she was drowning in sensual sensation, and she was almost relieved when he swung her up into his arms and carried her into the other room.

It wasn't until she felt the cool linen of the sofa cushions at her back that she realised her sweatpants were around her knees, but by then Alex had joined her. His hand took the place of his thigh between her legs, and she clutched the unbuttoned collar of his shirt when he found the moist petals that opened to his touch.

'Wait...'

Kate fumbled frantically with the rest of the buttons on his shirt and waistcoat, but although Alex allowed her to tear his shirt open he made no attempt to help her.

'Relax,' he told her roughly, bending to stroke her ear with his tongue, caressing the fluttering pulse he found there as his thumb caressed the sensitive nub between her legs.

Kate had barely pressed his shirt from his shoulders when her body convulsed, and she let out a little cry of anguish as wave upon wave of uncontrollable feeling swept over her. Her body throbbed around his fingers, soaking him with her heat, and he bent his head and covered her lips with his.

When she was capable of coherent thought again, Kate gazed at him with indignant eyes. 'That wasn't fair.'

'What wasn't fair?'

She moved her head from side to side, reaching for her sweatpants, trying to drag them up her legs. 'You—you didn't—'

'I know.' He prevented her from covering herself with very little effort. He shrugged. 'I don't have any protection. Besides, I wasn't sure you'd want—'

'Well, I did. I do,' she told him hotly. And, realising she had to prove it, she wriggled into a sitting position and reached for his belt. 'Take your clothes off.'

Alex's eyes darkened. 'What if someone comes—?'

'I've told you! My mother and Joanne won't be back for hours!' she exclaimed fiercely. 'Go on. I mean it. Take your clothes off.'

'All of them?' he asked mockingly, and she struggled onto her knees, kicking off her own sweatpants in the process.

'Yes,' she said huskily. 'I want to see you too.'

She thought he wasn't going to obey her, but she could see the pressure of his arousal swelling against his zip, and with a temerity she hadn't known she possessed she covered it with her hand.

His reaction was violent, and, holding her gaze with his, he unbuckled his belt and opened his zip. Beneath silk boxers, his thickness thrust into her hand, but he held her away from him while he disposed of the rest of his clothes.

'Don't,' he said hoarsely, and she could see how close to losing control he was.

It was then that she realised she was still wearing the top of her suit, and, peeling it off, she subsided against the cushions again. This time, Alex stretched his length beside her, and his mouth moved down her throat to her breasts. Although she was sure he was impatient to satisfy his own needs, he took the time to suckle each hard nipple, and she could feel herself getting aroused again by the hot hunger of his lips and teeth.

She almost stopped breathing altogether when he buried his face in the curls between her legs. But, apparently, there were limits to even his control, and when he moved over her again he nudged her legs apart.

She raised her knees as he knelt between them, and then he was pushing into her moist passage and her muscles were stretching, stretching to accommodate his length.

She ached at the unaccustomed invasion. It was so long since she'd been with a man, but it was heavenly, too, feeling Alex as a part of her at last. She wanted to wind her legs and arms around him, and keep him there inside her, but already other needs were demanding satisfaction.

'You're beautiful,' he muttered unsteadily, looking down at where their bodies were joined, and she uttered a quivery sigh.

'So are you,' she told him, and when he put his hand beneath her bottom and lifted her against him she eagerly wound her legs about his waist.

It was all over much too quickly. Almost as soon as Alex began to move, thrusting himself against her, her senses spun wildly out of control. And by the time he was shuddering with his own release rippling spasms of ecstasy were taking her up and up, ever higher, penetrating the very core of her being and tilting her into space...

CHAPTER TEN

ALEX drove back to Jamaica Hill feeling better than he'd felt in years. Maybe better than he'd ever felt before, he conceded ruefully, aware that he'd never been with a woman who responded so delightfully to his every touch.

And he'd wanted to touch her, he acknowledged now, right from the very first moment he'd seen her standing talking to Sam Guthrie. He'd known even then she was provocation, in tight leggings and a tweed jacket, and he mocked himself for the instantaneous way he'd responded to her appeal.

But, in the event, it had turned out that she had wanted him too, and in the aftermath of this evening's lovemaking she had admitted it. Indeed, they'd spent so long exploring one another's attraction that they had barely had time to get dressed again before her mother and Joanne had got back from Bath. That would have been something for the tabloids, he thought dryly. A picture of him and Kate cavorting on the sofa in her living room would just about finish him off.

An exaggeration, perhaps, but there was no doubt that the stables' recovery was a fragile thing at best, and another scurrilous piece of journalism was exactly what Conrad Wyatt needed to persuade a judge that he was totally amoral, and therefore no fit guardian for his daughter.

But, thankfully, that hadn't happened. Indeed, when Kate's daughter had found that he'd spent the evening with her mother she'd been gratifyingly positive about the whole affair.

'I knew it was your Range Rover that was parked downstairs!' Joanne had exclaimed, turning triumphantly to her grandmother. 'Didn't I say so, Nan?'

'You may have done so.'

Mrs Ross had been slightly less enthusiastic about his appearance, but Alex decided that was understandable. She hardly knew him, after all, and it was too soon to expect her to welcome him with open arms.

Too soon?

Alex frowned as he swung into the gates of Jamaica Hill. What did he mean by that? He surely wasn't seriously considering a permanent relationship on the basis of a couple of hours of good sex.

And that was all it had been, he assured himself firmly. Okay, it had been incredible sex, and Kate was every bit as desirable to him now as she had been earlier in the evening. But he was too old to start looking for constancy between a woman's legs. If his experiences with Pam had taught him anything it was that nothing was ever that simple.

But he liked Kate; he enjoyed her company. And, what was equally important, Rachel liked her, too. Despite the lateness of the hour, he'd taken the opportunity to ask Joanne if she'd like to come down to the stables some time when his daughter was there, and she'd been more than willing to accept his invitation. Indeed, he'd have gone so far as to say that Joanne had suspected that something had been going on between him and her mother, and her mischievous smile had not been entirely unbiased.

Which might be a reason for him to steer clear of Kate in future, he reflected dourly, his mood changing when, after leaving the Range Rover on the forecourt, he let himself into the house. He didn't want to give either of them the wrong impression, but when he thought of the consequences of not seeing Kate again he dismissed the alternative out of hand. He wanted to see her again; he intended to see her again; and, however reckless it might seem, he was prepared to take the risk.

Nevertheless, after he'd showered and slipped naked between the cool sheets on his bed, he determined not to take any further risks so far as unprotected sex was concerned. Kate had assured him she was unlikely to get pregnant at this particular time of the month, but there was always the danger that she could.

He groaned. God, why did the prospect of her having his baby not fill him with the dismay it should? Why did the very idea of his child swelling her stomach tighten his own? It was crazy but he wanted to make love to her again, sex against sex, skin against skin...

Despite his intentions to the contrary, he didn't see Kate again for a couple of days.

An owner, someone he'd dealt with for a number of years, and who had stuck with him throughout all the publicity surrounding Pamela's death, had phoned from the north of England. The man, who'd been attending a horse sale at a stud near York, had wanted Alex's opinion on a mare he'd seen there. He'd asked if there was any chance of Alex's driving north to join him, bringing a horse-box, if possible, to transport the animal back to Jamaica Hill should the sale go through.

It meant being away overnight and in other circumstances Alex might have asked Ted Lowes to go in his place. But the owner was a good friend, and a good customer, and he wasn't in the habit of asking for favours. In consequence, Alex felt obliged to go himself.

He considered ringing Kate before he left King's Montford, to explain where he was going and when he hoped to be back. But he didn't. He decided it might do them both good to have a breathing space before they saw one another again. It was probably better if he tried to cool it. Despite the warnings he'd given himself the night before, he was still far too eager to continue the affair.

Yet, as soon as he hit the M1, he started wishing he'd ignored his conscience. Kate was bound to wonder why he'd left town the morning after he'd visited the flat. So long as she didn't think he was avoiding her, he brooded irritably. Could he ring her from his hotel? What excuse could he give if her mother answered the phone?

In the event, he decided against doing anything so reckless. Guthrie would tell her where he was, he assured himself. Sam would explain the circumstances and he'd be back the following afternoon. He had to concentrate on his job, and on the fact that his solicitor was presently negotiating for him to have Rachel to stay for a whole weekend. His relationship with Kate—if they had a relationship—must not be allowed to interfere with his daughter's future.

Which was all very well. And, while he was discussing breeding schedules and blood lines, and deciding how much the mare he'd come to see was worth, he was almost able to convince himself he meant it. But, despite his concern for Rachel, he couldn't get Kate out of his thoughts, and in consequence he slept badly and awoke the next morning feeling heavy-eyed and depressed.

It didn't help that it was a lousy day, heavy rain making all driving a hazard. It was particularly frustrating to be driving a horse-box, which meant he had to limit his speed. He was eager to get back to King's Montford, but the weather slowed him down considerably. That, and the fact that an articulated wagon had jackknifed on the motorway, leaving a tailback of traffic five miles long.

He got soaked when he stopped to give the mare a breather, but he got himself a strong cup of coffee at the same time and that helped his headache a bit. But it was well into the evening before he reached his destination, and his head was throbbing so badly he felt physically sick.

Finding the gates to Jamaica Hill closed was another source of irritation. For God's sake, he thought, he'd told Ted Lowes he was driving back today. Why on earth would he close the gates?

It meant him getting out into the rain again to open them, and after getting back into the cab he drove straight down to the stables. Finding his head groom standing in the open doorway of the office, he was tempted to demand an explanation, but the man was looking edgy and Alex guessed he'd remembered what he'd done.

Instead, after exchanging the briefest of formalities, Alex grabbed his overcoat from the cab, and stamped across the paddock to the house. He was tired and not in the best of tempers. It was too late to contact Kate tonight and that was what was really bugging his mood.

He went straight into the library, and he was helping himself to a can of Coke when his housekeeper appeared. 'Och, thank God you're back!' she exclaimed, and he noticed how anxious she was looking. 'Could ye not have warned me ye'd be so late?'

It was a sign of her agitation that she'd relapsed into the dialect of her childhood, and Alex knew a moment's sympathy before his own resentment kicked in. 'I'm sorry,' he muttered. 'I didn't know I was under curfew. You try driving nearly three hundred miles in the pouring rain and see how accurate your timekeeping is.'

Mrs Muir twisted her hands together. 'You don't know, do you?' she cried. 'Ted didn't tell you that the police have been here?'

'The police!' Alex slammed down the can and turned to the old woman in disbelief. Then, in a whisper, he said, 'My God, something's happened to Rachel! Just tell me: has she had an accident, or what?'

'There's nothing wrong with Rachel—as far as I know,' Mrs Muir assured him hurriedly. 'The police came to interview you, Mr Kellerman.' She licked her lips rather nervously. 'They say that Mrs Sawyer has gone missing. No one's seen her since she left Jamaica Hill.'

'Alicia?' Alex blinked. 'They wanted to ask me about Alicia?' He relaxed a little. 'What does Alicia's disappearance have to do with me?'

'You may well ask.' The housekeeper grimaced. 'I told them we knew nothing about it. But I think they think they've found some evidence that connects with her disappearance. They asked when I'd last seen her.' She sniffed. 'I can't be sure, but I think they suspect something terrible has happened to her.'

Alex felt as if all the air in his lungs had been expelled in a rush and he couldn't seem to take in any more. Alicia, missing? He couldn't believe it, and he sank into the nearest chair, resting his arms on his spread thighs and dropping his head into his hands.

'Are you all right, Mr Kellerman?'

Mrs Muir was obviously anxious about him, and, bustling across to the refrigerated cabinet, she opened a bottle of mineral water and poured some into a glass.

'Drink this,' she said, tugging his arm and pushing the glass into his hand. 'Don't worry. They won't be back until tomorrow morning. I told them I didn't know what time you'd be home tonight.'

'Thanks.'

Alex took the glass and drank thirstily from it, the chilled water giving some relief to his pounding head. But, for God's sake, he thought, he'd hoped he was through with police interviews. Alicia couldn't be dead. And if she was, why the hell were they pointing the finger at him?

Of course, she had worked for him, and thanks to Conrad Wyatt there were still rumours circulating about the circumstances surrounding Pamela's death. Hell, the old man would be clapping his hands in delight if this was made public. How was he ever going to get Rachel back if this became another *cause célèbre*?

'You're going to have to tell them,' said Mrs Muir suddenly, and his head swung up to face her.

'Tell them what?' he demanded harshly. 'You don't think I had anything to do with Alicia's disappearance, do you?'

'Of course not.' The old housekeeper was impatient. 'You forget: I know how that woman used to pursue you. It was because you'd have nothing to do with her that she walked out.'

'Who's going to believe that now?'

'Well, I do.' Mrs Muir put her hand on his shoulder and squeezed gently. 'I mean, you're going to have to tell them about Jim,' she declared steadily. 'You've protected us both for far too long, and I can't let you go on destroying your-self.'

'Oh, Agnes...' Alex tipped back his head and flexed his shoulders wearily. 'I don't think the police will believe any-thing I say at this point in time. Let's hope they find Alicia, or that she hears what's going on and comes forward herself. Until that happens, it looks like I'm their prime suspect.'

'But it's not fair.'

'No.' Alex conceded the point, getting to his feet and set-ting the empty glass on the corner of his desk. 'Did they say what this new evidence was, or who'd drawn their attention to it? Do you think it's possible that Pam's father's in-volved?'

'I don't know.' Mrs Muir bent her head. 'But there's some-thing else I haven't told you, Mr Kellerman.'

'What?' Alex gazed at her, narrow-eyed. 'Don't tell me they've found a body as well?'

'No.' The housekeeper pursed her lips. 'But they told me her husband—'

'Henry Sawyer?'

'Yes. He apparently reported her missing.'

'So?'

'Well—they said he'd used the services of a private in-vestigator here in town to corroborate his suspicions.'

'So?' Alex shook his head. 'I didn't even know there was a private detective agency in King's Montford.' And then, seeing the old woman's expression, he asked, 'Are you say-ing that I've spoken to this—investigator myself?'

'Oh, yes.' Mrs Muir backed up a bit, as if she feared an explosion. 'She—she's been working here for the past three weeks, Mr Kellerman. I'm afraid—I'm afraid it's Mrs Hughes.'

Alex eventually crawled into bed but he didn't sleep. In fact, he didn't know how he restrained himself from getting back into the car and driving to Milner Court to confront Kate, late as it was. Every nerve in his body was crying out for retribution, for the chance to tell her what a deceitful bitch he thought she was.

Yet it was hard to accept that what Mrs Muir had said was gospel. Had Kate really tricked him, and tantalised him, and reduced him to an emotional wreck, just to satisfy some perverted belief of Henry Sawyer's that he was responsible for his wife's disappearance? That was what hurt the most—the fact that she'd taken some other man's word as to his character. He'd put his daughter's life on hold while he made love to a woman who'd been sent to destroy him.

Which meant everything they'd shared had been a mockery. She'd probably encouraged his interest in the hope of hearing some incriminatory pillow talk from him. His fist slammed into his pillow. God, did she really suspect that he was capable of murder? And if so, hadn't she taken an enormous risk by letting him into her flat when she was alone?

He didn't know and he tried to tell himself he didn't care when he hauled himself out of bed the following morning. Dammit, he had more to worry about than the circumstances behind why he'd got laid. The police were coming back this morning to interview him, and, remembering their diligence two years ago, he doubted they'd care whether he'd had breakfast or not.

Not that he wanted anything to eat, he thought, his stomach churning nauseously. Despite the fact that he hadn't had a decent meal since dinner two nights ago, Alex couldn't face the thought of food. Caffeine was what he needed, and much against Mrs Muir's advice he drank several cups of strong black coffee, so that by the time the detective inspector and his sidekick were shown into the library he felt as hyper as an addict on crack.

The interview was fairly short. Detective Inspector Rivers, a dapper individual wearing a slightly shiny suit, seemed very much concerned with his own importance, and he looked around the library as he came in, as if assessing how much Alex might have gained from his late wife's death. He hadn't been on that case, but that didn't matter. Alex guessed he'd have read through the files before coming here.

The inspector's first question was predictable. He asked when Alex had last seen Alicia Sawyer, and then, under what circumstances had she left his employ? Speaking quietly, Alex explained that Mrs Sawyer had not found the work to her liking and that, after a short period, she'd decided to leave.

'It was Mrs Sawyer's decision to terminate her employment, was it, sir?' The inspector's question was polite enough, but Alex thought he could hear the veiled insolence in his voice.

'No, it was mine,' he said, refusing to compromise about Alicia's departure. 'We—had a difference of opinion, and she walked out.'

'And when did this row take place, sir?'

'It wasn't a row.' Alex balled his fists, and in his ear he could hear Kate telling him to lighten up. She'd implied he was his own worst enemy, and it was probably true. He showed his real feelings too well.

'But you admit you did have an argument, Mr Kellerman,' suggested the detective constable, only to fall silent again when his superior sent him a glowering look.

'We had a difference of opinion,' Alex repeated, breathing deeply. 'I've no idea where she went after she left here.'

'She left no forwarding address?'

'No.'

'She had no friends here who might know where she's gone?'

'You'd have to ask the men,' said Alex, mentally dreading the thought of another investigation into his life. 'If that's all—er—Sergeant—'

'It's not. And it's *Detective Inspector* Rivers, Mr Kellerman.' The dour little man scowled, and Alex hoped he wouldn't regret the urge to put him down. 'There's been another development; you might say, a rather serious development, Mr Kellerman. Mrs Sawyer's suitcases have been found. At the bottom of a rubbish skip in town.'

Alex could feel the colour draining out of his face. 'I see,' he said, and he knew his voice was strained. But, for God's sake, Alicia's suitcases in a rubbish tip! 'Who—who found them?' he asked, hoping he didn't sound as guilty as he felt.

'Some children,' replied Rivers, watching him closely. 'Do you have any idea how the suitcases got into the tip, Mr Kellerman?'

'Of course not.' Alex was appalled. But he was aware that they didn't believe him. Yet how was he supposed to act when he was apparently the last person to see her—what? Alive?

'I understand you've been away.'

Rivers was speaking again, and Alex struggled to answer him. 'That's right,' he said, wondering if they really suspected he'd been disposing of the body. 'Um—I've been in York,' he added. 'With one of my owners. We bought a horse: an Arabian. I brought it back to Jamaica Hill.'

'In a horse-box, Mr Kellerman?'

'Of course.' Alex could only guess what he was thinking.

'I see.' Rivers drew himself up to his full height and attempted to look Alex in the face. 'I assume this—owner—can confirm your whereabouts for the past two days?'

'If necessary.' Alex's jaw clamped at the prospect of having to ask someone else to vouch that he was telling the truth. 'Now, will that be all? I do have quite a lot of work to catch up on.'

'So long as you don't go away again, sir,' said Detective Inspector Rivers crisply. 'At the moment we're trying to find out how long the suitcases have been in the skip, so we may need to speak to you again.'

'I didn't put them there,' said Alex, forcing himself not to react to the inspector's attitude. 'But I'll be here.' He took another steadying breath. 'I'm sorry I couldn't be of any more help.'

Alex waited until Mrs Muir had shown the two men out

before flinging himself into the leather chair behind his desk.
'Bastard,' he muttered harshly, levelling his gaze on the half-
full decanter of Scotch residing on the top of the cabinet at
the other side of the room. Who in hell would have put
Alicia's suitcases in the rubbish skip? Remembering how
particular she'd been about her appearance, he couldn't believe she'd do something like that herself.

Then who?

And why?

One name sprang into his mind instantly. But would his
father-in-law go as far as to hire a private detective to find a
woman he knew only by reputation? It didn't make sense.
When he'd met Kate at Wyvern Hall, there'd been no recognition there. Unless they were both better actors than he
was giving them credit for. But Kate had defended him to
Conrad. Would she have done that if the old man was paying
her fee?

Kate…

The thought of what she'd done to him was a painful torment. The Scotch looked even more of a temptation with her
on his mind. It would be so easy to give in, so easy to pour
himself a glass of the rich dark malt and let the alcohol dull
his senses. Dear God, was it only forty-eight hours ago that
he'd begun to believe he might have a future, after all?

'They've gone.' Mrs Muir stood in the open doorway gazing anxiously at him. 'Well? Are you going to tell me what
they had to say?'

Alex's shoulders slumped. 'They've found Alicia's belongings; her suitcases. Someone has dumped them in a rubbish skip in town.'

'What?' Mrs Muir looked totally staggered. 'So that's why
they've started an investigation. Did Mr Sawyer find them?
Is that why he—?'

'Some children apparently found them,' Alex interrupted
her heavily. 'As far as I know, they don't know how long
they may have been lying there. They probably think I
dumped them after I'd got rid of her body.'

Mrs Muir gasped in horror. 'They're surely not accusing you of having anything to do with her disappearance?'

'Well, not yet,' said Alex flatly. 'Give them time.'

'But—that's ridiculous.' Mrs Muir was angry. 'What about her husband? She always said he resented you giving her a room here. Isn't it far more likely that he's involved?'

'She also said that he used to beat her,' Alex reminded her. 'And we soon found out that that wasn't true.' He grimaced. 'It's not up to me to accuse anyone else of being involved. I've had enough of that myself.'

'But it was Mr Sawyer who hired—well, the private detective, wasn't it?'

'Was it?'

Mrs Muir frowned. 'You're not thinking that Mrs Hughes herself—'

'No.' Alex scowled at the mention of Kate's name, and continued harshly, 'I mean Wyatt. Perhaps I'm getting too close to persuading the authorities that Rachel belongs with me, and this is his way of scaring them off.'

'By getting rid of Mrs Sawyer?'

Mrs Muir looked alarmed now, and Alex pulled a wry face. 'No,' he said impatiently. 'By using her disappearance to implicate me. Perhaps those weren't her suitcases at all. If Henry Sawyer identified them they could be anybody's.'

'Oh, yes, I see.' Mrs Muir nodded. 'So you think they might have put her name inside?'

'How else were they able to identify them?' asked Alex practically. He glanced at his watch. 'It's time I found out. Mrs Hughes should be arriving soon.'

'Oh, Mr Kellerman, is that wise?' Mrs Muir gazed at him dubiously. 'She may not come in, of course, but I'd stay away from that young woman if I were you.'

'But you're not me, Mrs Muir,' declared Alex, his eyes glittering malevolently. He cast one last look at the Scotch, and got to his feet. 'Get rid of that whisky, will you? I have the feeling I'm going to need all my faculties about me to survive the next few days.'

CHAPTER ELEVEN

KATE wondered why she'd allowed Joanne to accompany her to the stables that morning. She knew Alex was due back from York today, and he obviously wouldn't be expecting her to have taken him up on his offer so soon. Apart from anything else, he would probably be too busy to come down to the yard, and she'd be left with the awkward task of having to explain his invitation to Mr Guthrie.

Joanne, of course, was delighted. Apart from the fact that it was a special treat, she'd have done anything if it meant getting out of the flat. And she had worked reasonably well at the schoolwork Mr Coulthard had had her teachers send home for her. Kate supposed she deserved the break. She just wished she'd waited until she'd spoken to Alex again.

But, if she was honest, that was one of the reasons why she'd given in to Joanne's pleading. She hadn't seen Alex since the night before he went to York, and the truth was, she was half afraid he might have regretted what had happened at the flat. She had been the instigator, after all, however eager Alex might have been to play along with her. What if he'd never intended things to go that far? What if he really had just come to speak to Joanne, as he'd said?

And, in all honesty, she was appalled at her own conduct. She'd never been the kind of woman to do anything more than indulge in a light flirtation with a man. Apart from Sean, her experience with men was limited. Which made what she'd done so totally out of character for her.

And, during the last couple of days, she'd struggled to find a reason for her wanton behaviour. Just remembering how she'd thrown herself at Alex could still bring a film of sweat to her brow. But she'd never known what it was like to actually desire a man before; to need his touch so badly that she wanted to get under his skin.

Instead of which, he'd got under hers, she acknowledged ruefully, a pulse in the pit of her stomach reminding her of the restless nights she'd spent since he went away. If she allowed herself to think of him at all, she got an actual ache between her legs, and she'd taken so many cold showers, her mother was beginning to think she'd got a fever.

And she had, she admitted tensely as they approached the entrance to Jamaica Hill. But it wasn't a fever that she could cure with drugs. She'd fallen in love with Alex Kellerman. He was the fever in her blood. And, as soon as they were alone together, she was going to tell him the truth.

Which was another reason why she'd brought Joanne along this morning. She fully expected him to be furious with her when she told him she was a private investigator, but she hoped he might be more tolerant if her daughter was there. She'd asked Susie to make up the account, severing her connection with Henry Sawyer, and if Alex fired her, as she expected he would, she'd have to go back to investigating insurance claims and try to forget him.

There were some people gathered outside the gates to the estate. The gates were closed, which was unusual, but she didn't recognise the two men and one woman who were hanging about outside. She slowed, feeling a surge of apprehension when she noticed that two of them were carrying cameras, and when Joanne turned a puzzled look in her direction she said, 'You get out and open the gates, Jo. And don't answer any questions, do you hear?'

But when Joanne got out, leaving the door of the car open, it was Kate who had to suffer an onslaught of questions about who she was and what she was doing there. 'You work for Alex Kellerman, right?' demanded the woman pushily. 'What's your opinion about Mrs Sawyer's suitcases turning up?'

Kate blanched, but although she was dying to ask what the woman meant she kept her mouth shut. But, 'Mrs

Sawyer's suitcases'? she thought, shaking her head confusedly. What on earth were they talking about? And where had the cases been found?

Surely not here!

She leant across and slammed the door, before the woman could push into the car, and then drove through the gates when Joanne opened them. Joanne closed the gates again, ignoring the questions they threw at her now, and then scrambled into the car with an anxious look on her face.

'What's going on, Mum?'

'I wish I knew.' But Kate was feeling more and more uneasy. If it was true that they'd found Alicia's belongings, then obviously Alex must have been interviewed when he got back from York. Why else would the reporters—for that was what they were—be camping on his doorstep? She swallowed. Oh, God, what else might he have found out?

She half expected his car to be standing in the yard, but it wasn't. And no one gave her and Joanne any suspicious looks as she parked her car. Indeed, the work of the stables seemed to be proceeding as normal, were it not for a certain tension in the air.

Which probably only she was conscious of, she told herself impatiently as she and Joanne crossed the yard and went into her office. Even the electric fire was glowing cheerfully, and the mail was piled on her desk, as usual, waiting for her attention.

The phone rang before she had had time to check whether Mr Guthrie was in his office. To her alarm, it was Susie, and she knew something must have happened because her assistant had been warned never to contact her here.

'What is it?' she asked, keeping a wary eye on her daughter as she spoke. She knew Joanne must be curious about what was going on, but she couldn't discuss Alex's affairs with her.

'The police have been here!' exclaimed Susie, her voice high and agitated. 'They wanted to see you, and I had to tell them where I thought you were.'

'What, here?' Kate pressed a hand to her chest where her heart was beating erratically.

'That's right.' Susie was distraught. 'There was nothing else I could do. I couldn't tell lies.'

'No.' Kate conceded the point, her mind racing madly. Were the police already here? she wondered. Dear God, Alex would blow his top if he found out why they wanted to see her. She had to try and speak to him before they arrived, but that wasn't going to be easy. She had no way of knowing whether he intended to come down to the yard today.

'They've found that woman's luggage,' continued Susie, interrupting her abstraction. 'Some children found two suitcases in a skip.'

'A skip!' Kate was horrified. 'My God, have they found a body?'

'Not yet,' said a cold, sardonic voice behind her, and she swung round to find Alex propped in the open doorway of Mr Guthrie's office. 'But I'm sure they think it's just a matter of time.'

Kate's jaw sagged. Her mouth opened and closed as she struggled with the dilemma of how to answer Alex with Susie's faintly hysterical voice still chattering in her ear.

But, in the event, Joanne saved the situation for her. 'Hello, Mr Kellerman,' she greeted him brightly. 'I hope you don't mind. Mum said it would probably be all right if I came to the stables today.' She gestured towards her mother. 'Mum—Mum's just speaking to—to a friend—'

'Is she?' Kate told Susie she would ring her back, and replaced the receiver before he spoke again. 'Well—why don't you go and have a look around while I have a few words with your mother?' He pointed through the window. 'See that young man there: that's Billy Roach, one of the apprentices. If you tell him who you are, he'll give you a guided tour.'

Joanne hesitated, looking half anxiously at her mother. 'Will you—will that be all right, Mum?' she asked, and Kate guessed she'd picked up on the atmosphere between her and Alex, which she was sure you could have cut with a knife.

'Yes,' she said, her throat tight. 'You'll like Billy. He's a nice boy. He's always been very friendly with me.'

'And what could be a higher recommendation?' asked Alex sarcastically. He turned back into Guthrie's office. 'Will you come in here, Mrs Hughes?'

'Mum—'

Joanne still looked troubled, but Kate knew she couldn't let her daughter get involved in her problems. 'Go on,' she said. 'You'll enjoy yourself.'

'But will you be all right?'

Joanne's nod towards the inner office was uneasy. 'I'll be fine,' Kate assured her firmly, wishing she felt as confident as she sounded.

With Joanne gone, Kate walked apprehensively to the open doorway, glancing in to find Alex was standing staring out of the window as before. 'Sit down,' he said, and this time she obeyed him. Maybe her stomach would stop turning cartwheels if she took the weight off her legs.

The silence that followed was ominous, and Kate's stomach started churning all over again. Oh, God, she thought, why couldn't she think of something to say in her own defence? She'd been doing a job, earning a living, just like anyone else.

'Who hired you?'

Alex's question came as something of an anticlimax. She'd expected him to accuse her of deceiving him, of using his apparent attraction towards her for her own ends. But perhaps that hadn't been as important to him as it had been to her. His pride was hurt, but probably nothing else.

'Henry—Henry Sawyer,' she said now, realising she was breaking a confidence, and he swung round to face her with malevolent eyes.

'You expect me to believe that?' he snarled, and she quickly revised her estimates of his emotions. Alex was angry, and she felt a twinge of fear as he stalked round the desk towards her.

'It's the truth,' she got out quickly, trying not to let him see her feelings. 'He told me his wife had disappeared. I thought it would be a fairly straightforward investigation.'

'Investigation!' Alex made the word sound dirty. 'Well, forgive me for sounding sceptical, but you don't seem to have done a great deal to earn your fee. I assume this man— Sawyer—did pay you? I always wondered how you managed to live on what you earned here.'

Kate sighed. 'It's a job, Al—Mr Kellerman. And, yes, he paid me.'

'Not a lot, I trust,' said Alex harshly. 'You don't appear to have succeeded in your quest.'

'No.' Kate's lips tightened. 'I—I told Mr Sawyer I had no idea where his wife went after she left here. But I made all the usual enquiries. I earned my money, Mr Kellerman.'

'How?' Alex put one hand on either arm of her chair now and thrust his face towards her. 'By seducing your client's suspect, I assume.'

'No.' Kate's face burned, but his means of belittling her caught her on the raw. 'I earn a hundred pounds a day, plus expenses. Someone must think I do a decent job.'

Alex released the chair and stepped back, his expression staggered. 'You're saying Sawyer paid you that kind of money to look for his wife?'

'Yes.' Kate swallowed. 'It's the going rate at the moment. I explained that to him before I took the job.'

Alex's dark brows descended. 'And has he paid you?'

'That's my business—' she began, but the fury in his face caused her to break off. 'All right, yes,' she conceded. 'I always ask for an advance payment. Otherwise a client might not want to pay if—if—'

'If you foul up?' Alex was disparaging. Then he said, 'So tell me, where would Sawyer find—what? A thousand pounds?—when he's out of a job?'

Kate decided not to admit how much Henry Sawyer had

paid her. Then, as her brain kicked into gear, she asked, 'What are you saying? That you think someone else put Sawyer up to it? Someone else gave him the cash?'

Alex raked back his hair with an angry hand. 'What do you think?' he snapped. Then, his lips twisting, he added, 'But I forgot: you're in on this, too. You probably know damn well who financed this little conspiracy. But I have to give it to you—you'd never have guessed it from the way you stood up to him last week.'

Kate pushed herself up from her chair. 'You're saying you think—your father-in-law is behind it?'

'Who else?' Alex gave her a savage look. 'Well, he certainly knew how to bait his hook!'

'Me?' Kate was indignant. 'I had nothing to do with him. I was getting nowhere with the investigation and Sawyer—Sawyer brought the advertisement for this job to me and suggested I apply.'

'Why?'

'Why?' Kate licked her lips before replying. 'Well, his original claim was that you and she had had an affair.'

'An affair?'

'Yes.' Kate tried to ignore his stunned expression and continued doggedly, 'He said that he and his wife were happy until she came to work for you.'

Alex shook his head. 'And you believed him, I suppose.'

'I had no reason not to.' Kate hesitated. 'Well, not then. You were a stranger to me.'

'A stranger who everyone suspected of murdering his wife,' put in Alex bitterly. 'Oh, I bet you and Sawyer had some cosy discussions about what went on at Jamaica Hill.'

'That's not true.' Kate knew she couldn't let him go on thinking that. 'As a matter of fact, I didn't tell him anything about you at all. That—that's probably why he was threatening to ask for his money back.' She took a breath. 'You have to believe me. I was going to withdraw from the investigation today.'

Alex snorted. 'You expect me to believe that?'

'It's true.' She touched his sleeve. 'I was hoping you might forgive me. After—after what happened between us—'

'The good sex, you mean?' asked Alex crudely, moving so that her arm fell to her side. 'Please, don't perjure yourself on my account. Remember, you've only my word that I didn't have an affair with Alicia. Perhaps I did. Perhaps I killed her as well.' He caught her chin with cruel fingers, and bent to assault her mouth with a hard, punishing kiss. 'Face it, Kate, you're never going to find out the truth!'

'Oh, I think she will.' The cool, invasive voice caused Alex to release her abruptly, but she thought the oath he uttered was only audible to her. 'We meet again, Mr Kellerman,' the hateful voice continued. 'Rather sooner than I had anticipated. But, don't worry, on this occasion I've come to interview Mrs Hughes.'

'I'm sure nothing you did could worry me, Inspector,' said Alex insolently, and Kate groaned inwardly at the dangerous light in his eyes. 'And, if you'll excuse me, I, too, have matters to attend to.' He looked at Kate. 'Places to go, people to see.'

A shadow appeared in the office doorway as Kate was clearing her desk. For a moment she thought—*hoped*—that it might be Alex, that he might have thought better of his accusations and decided to listen to what she had to say. She couldn't believe—wouldn't believe—that he could dismiss what had happened between them so derisively. He was angry, with good reason, but he had to know that she believed in him.

She was so afraid he was going to do something stupid, like going to see Conrad Wyatt, and confronting him with his suspicions about Alicia's disappearance. God knew, Wyatt had done his best to provoke his anger when he'd gone to pick up his daughter last week. In the present situation, Alex couldn't afford to give the police a reason to believe he was a violent man.

But it wasn't Alex, she saw at once, her heart sinking. It

was Mrs Sheridan, the woman who owned the estate that adjoined Jamaica Hill. The woman who Alex had said was a good friend—though she didn't look particularly friendly at the moment. Had she heard why Kate had been working at the stables? Had she come to add her accusations to the rest?

'If you're looking for Mr Kellerman, he's not here, Mrs Sheridan,' said Kate bluntly, deciding there was no point in pretending she didn't know who she was.

'I know.' Lacey came into the office and closed the door, leaning back against it. 'It was you I wanted to speak to, Mrs—Hughes, isn't it? Alex is out at present. I don't think Mrs Muir knows when he'll be back.'

Alex was out!

Kate wanted to groan with frustration. Had he gone to Wyvern Hall? Oh, God, she fretted, if he had she should have gone with him. But she knew he'd never have allowed her to do it, even if she'd begged him to take her along.

Meanwhile, Lacey was looking round the office. She was an attractive woman, Kate thought reluctantly, though obviously much older than she'd like everyone to believe. Her shoulder-length bob was expertly tinted, and the vee of her suit jacket was cut low enough to give a tantalising glimpse of her impressive cleavage.

'Do I take it you're leaving?' Lacey asked, nodding towards the box of personal belongings the other woman had set on the desk, and Kate sighed impatiently.

'That's right,' she said, bending over the box again, determined not to discuss the terms of her employment with Lacey. 'If you'd like to tell me what you want? As you can see, I am rather busy right now.'

'I gather Alex has fired you?'

'Not exactly.' But Kate could feel the hot colour entering her cheeks at Lacey's sardonic words.

'But you are leaving,' Lacey pointed out. 'Are you saying that it's your decision? I find it hard to believe after what he told me last night.'

Kate lifted her head. She knew Lacey wanted her to ask what Alex had said about her, but she wouldn't give her the satisfaction of knowing she cared. 'Does it matter?' she asked instead, knowing it was a cop-out. 'Is that why you came, Mrs Sheridan? To make sure I left the premises?'

Lacey shook her head and straightened away from the door. 'No,' she said smoothly. 'I just wanted to give you a warning. If you care anything for Alex, you'll take my advice and stay out of his life.'

Kate did look at her now. 'Are you threatening me, Mrs Sheridan?' Her heart was thumping and there was a sense of unreality about this whole scene. For heaven's sake, Lacey Sheridan had to be nearer fifty than forty. Was she implying she had some emotional influence in Alex's life?

'No. Just warning you,' responded Lacey carelessly. 'Alex and I go back a long way, and I've no intention of allowing some trashy little secretary to come between us now. What I'm saying, Mrs Hughes, is that Alex and I are lovers.' She was so close to Kate now that Kate could smell the other woman's heavy perfume mingling with the heat of her body. 'I wouldn't want you to get the wrong idea.'

To Kate's relief, Joanne chose that moment to come bursting into the office. 'Hey, Mum!' she was exclaiming, her excitement evident in her voice. 'You'll never guess what Billy said—'

She broke off in some confusion when she saw her mother wasn't alone, and Lacey turned towards her with an irritated expression. 'Didn't anybody ever teach you to knock on doors before opening them?' she snapped.

Joanne seemed hesitant for a moment, but then she looked at her mother and saw Kate's strained face. She immediately adopted her most insolent attitude, and, placing her hands on her hips, she responded, 'No, they didn't. And this is Mr Kellerman's office, not yours. You've got no right to tell me what to do.'

It was almost lunchtime before Kate got to her office. Susie had already left to meet her current boyfriend, and Kate sank gratefully into the chair behind her desk. What a day! she thought. What a nightmare! The only bright spot was Joanne's rout of Lacey Sheridan.

Not that Kate hadn't reproved her daughter for it. But it had been so nice to have someone taking her side for a change. After the things Alex had said, the scathing way he had dismissed their relationship, she had felt raw and used, and hearing that woman, that flashy woman, telling her that she and Alex were lovers had been the final straw.

And she had had the nerve to call Kate a 'trashy secretary'. As if she looked as if she'd ever done an honest day's work in her life! Even the clothes she'd worn had been more suitable for a woman half her age. She was a sad and jealous woman and Kate was secretly glad that Joanne had pricked her bubble of conceit.

What had hurt most, though, was hearing Lacey declare that she and Alex had a relationship. It meant that what he'd scornfully described as 'good sex' had not been said in the heat of the moment. He'd meant every word.

Of course, Lacey had taken umbrage at Joanne's words, and walked out threatening to tell Alex what had been going on, but that could hardly matter in the circumstances. Kate wondered if she'd threatened Alicia Sawyer too, it might explain why the other woman had left Jamaica Hill so precipitately. Left without leaving a forwarding address.

And then there'd been that interview with Detective Inspector Rivers. She hadn't liked the man, or his questions, though she supposed he was just doing his job. Not that she could help him with his investigations. She could only reiterate what she'd told Alex himself. She'd been doing a job— and not very successfully. She hoped the inspector hadn't suspected she'd let her personal feelings get in the way of objectivity where Alicia's disappearance was concerned.

Alicia...

Kate sniffed. She wished she'd never heard of Alicia. If she hadn't, she'd never have met Alex Kellerman or got involved in his personal affairs. She found no comfort in the old saying that it was better to have loved and lost than never to have loved at all.

She frowned and, unlocking the drawer at the side of the desk, she drew out the folder that contained all the details of the case. Her notes were there, along with the accounts she'd kept of her interviews with Billy Roach and Mrs Muir, and the snapshot Henry Sawyer had given her of his wife.

She scowled at the smudgy picture, then, reaching into the drawer again, she pulled out her eye-glass. She thought its magnifying lens might give her a clearer image of the missing woman, and when she turned on the lamp over the desk Alicia's face came slowly into focus.

But the photograph was still blurry, giving more of an impression of her appearance than anything else. Her face was there, a very attractive face as she'd recognised originally, her cloud of blonde hair serving to soften her rather sharp features.

They were almost hostile features, thought Kate, wondering why she suddenly felt that that was important. She had the strangest feeling that she'd seen that face before. Well, she had. She grimaced impatiently. In the beginning, she'd studied it to distraction. Her mind was simply creating a memory of that.

Or was it?

She chewed on her lower lip. She was sure she'd seen that face, and recently. But where? And in what connection? It didn't make sense. She tried to think. Apart from the supermarket and the snack bar, when she'd been with Alex and his daughter, she'd hardly got a social life.

She blew out a breath. It was so frustrating. Not as frustrating as Alex's dealings with his in-laws, perhaps, but close. *His in-laws!* Kate's breath caught somewhere in her throat and she strove for air. God Almighty, she breathed, when she'd recovered, that was where she'd seen Alicia. It hadn't been Mrs Wyatt she'd glimpsed peering through the window at Wyvern Hall. As crazy as it seemed she was almost sure it had been *her*!

CHAPTER TWELVE

'THERE'S a lady to see you, Kate.' Susie stood blocking the doorway to her employer's office, glancing somewhat doubtfully over her shoulder. 'She says it's urgent,' she added. And then, in a stage whisper, 'She says her name's Mrs Muir.'

Mrs Muir!

Kate got abruptly to her feet. 'Um—show her in, Susie,' she said, ignoring the younger woman's efforts to mime her disapproval. 'Go on. She won't bite.'

Susie pulled a resigned face and turned back into the office behind her. 'Mrs Hughes will see you now,' she said, her offhand tone reminiscent of Joanne's. 'Go straight in.'

'Thank you.'

Mrs Muir's gentle brogue was unmistakable, and Kate found herself growing tense despite her confident words to Susie. She couldn't imagine what Alex's housekeeper could want with her.

Mrs Muir came into the office looking almost as nervous as Kate. 'Good morning, Mrs Hughes,' she said, holding out her hand for Kate to shake, just as if she were an ordinary client. 'It's so nice to see you again.'

'Is it?' Kate couldn't help the query, but happily Mrs Muir didn't seem to think it required an answer. Susie was still hovering, so Kate asked her if she'd bring them a tray of tea. 'I'm afraid the coffee is fairly unpalatable,' she added to her visitor as she sat down again.

Mrs Muir had already subsided into the chair opposite, and now she took the time to set her handbag on the floor beside her chair. 'It's a chilly day,' she said. 'Did you have a good Christmas? I expect your daughter enjoyed the celebrations.'

Kate took a deep breath. 'I'm sure you didn't come here to talk about Joanne, Mrs Muir,' she said politely. 'I'd appreciate it if you could tell me what you want.' She rustled the papers on her desk, which were actually bills, but her visitor wasn't to know that. 'I am rather busy…'

'Of course, of course.' Mrs Muir nodded her grey head understandingly. 'I'm sure your success in finding Mrs Sawyer must have brought you a lot of extra business. And I don't want to hold you up. Not at all. But I really felt I had to come and see you and tell you how much I appreciate what you've done for Mr Kellerman.'

Kate expelled the breath she'd hardly been aware she was holding, and then looked up with some relief when Susie came bustling in with the tray. 'I couldn't find any biscuits, Mrs Hughes, so I popped next door and bought a couple of doughnuts.' She pulled a face at Kate's expression. 'I know they're fattening, but you could do with putting on some weight.'

'Yes, you do appear to have lost a little weight, Mrs Hughes.' Mrs Muir took up Susie's comment after the girl had left the room.

'I've—not been feeling very hungry,' said Kate shortly, not wanting to get into personal matters. 'And there was no need for you to come and see me, Mrs Muir. Mr Kellerman's solicitor wrote me a very nice letter of acknowledgement when the police charged Conrad Wyatt with bribery, and conspiracy, and goodness knows what else.'

In fact, as far as Kate was concerned, finding Alicia Sawyer had been something of an anticlimax in the end. The police—especially Inspector Rivers—mightn't have wanted to believe her when she went to them with her suspicions, but Henry Sawyer had proved pathetically eager to co-operate when confronted by the law. It turned out he had worked for Conrad Wyatt years ago and had been dismissed for stealing. It had been a simple matter for Wyatt to remind him of that previous misdemeanour, and threaten him with legal proceedings if Sawyer refused to co-operate with him.

And, of course, he hadn't. Kate didn't know all the details, but somehow Wyatt had convinced both Sawyer and his estranged wife that it would be in their interests to assist him in his plans. She guessed a considerable amount of money must have changed hands. Remembering the two sums Henry Sawyer had given her, she doubted Wyatt would have quibbled over their fee. He'd obviously intended the rumours to spread about Alicia's disappearance just as they had when Pamela had died. Whether he'd ever intended to produce Alicia again was anyone's guess. Kate thought it more likely that when the job was done, and Alex was discredited—yet again—both Alicia and her husband would have been given passports to a more luxurious life overseas.

Kate found the fact that Henry Sawyer had once worked for the Wyatts particularly galling. It had never occurred to her to investigate him, or to connect Alicia's disappearance with Alex's in-laws until she'd examined the photograph again. She was sure an experienced investigator would have seen the connection immediately, particularly after Alex had expressed his suspicions about his father-in-law.

In the event, Conrad's arrest and subsequent charges had proved a nine-day wonder. The local papers had made a big thing of his attempted efforts to destroy his son-in-law's character, but the national papers had barely taken it up. An earthquake in South America and sabre-rattling in the Middle East had driven the story into virtual insignificance, and Kate had thought how unfair it was that nobody had bothered to point out that it had been Conrad Wyatt's allegations at the time of his daughter's death that had caused Alex so much grief.

'His solicitor!' Mrs Muir sounded dismayed now. 'Mr Kellerman had Julian Morris write to you on his behalf?'

'That's right.' Kate sighed and poured the tea. 'But don't look like that. It's not important.' Well, not to him, obviously. 'I wasn't working for Mr Kellerman, after all.'

'All the same...' Mrs Muir was clearly upset by this disclosure. 'I honestly thought he'd been to see you himself.'

'No.' Kate pushed a cup of tea towards Mrs Muir and

gestured towards the doughnuts, which were oozing jam all over the plate. 'Please, help yourself.'

Mrs Muir shook her head. 'The tea is fine,' she said, and Kate agreed with her. The sight of the sticky buns was making her feel sick. But then, most things made her feel sick at the moment, and she hoped when the nausea passed she'd feel more optimistic about the future.

Mrs Muir took a sip of her tea and then replaced the cup on its saucer. Then she bent and lifted her bag into her lap and took a clean white tissue out of a plastic case. She used the tissue to blow her nose before tucking it back into the bag.

The whole operation took several minutes, and Kate had the feeling that it was deliberate. She wondered if Mrs Muir had some other reason for coming here, other than to offer her appreciation of what she'd supposedly done for Alex. Did the housekeeper have a problem? Should she explain that after breaching Henry Sawyer's confidence—however justified it might have been—she intended closing the agency next week?

Mrs Muir took another sip of her tea, and Kate could feel her nerves tightening. It wasn't that she didn't like the little woman, but she wasn't in the mood for social chit-chat today. She was glad that the housekeeper apparently bore her no ill will for deceiving Alex into employing her, but she doubted she was ever likely to see her again.

'Um—' she began, hoping to prompt some kind of action, and Mrs Muir straightened in her seat and pressed her hands together in her lap.

'You'll be wondering what more I could possibly have to say,' she said, as if she could read Kate's mind. 'Well, I thought it was time I told—someone—the truth.'

'The truth?' Kate stared at her, her mind buzzing with half-formed ideas she didn't want to face.

'About Mrs Kellerman's death,' said Mrs Muir. 'It—wasn't an accident. Well, it was,' she hastened on confus-

ingly, 'but that horse was deliberately put into the wrong
stall.'

Kate felt the bile rise in the back of her throat. 'You mean,
Alex—'

'Alex didn't do it.' Mrs Muir was vehement. 'It was my
husband that did it, Mrs Hughes. My Jim.' She groped for
the tissue again, and pressed it to her nose in obvious anguish. 'He wanted to hurt Pamela, you see, but he never
expected she'd be killed.'

Kate was staggered. 'You mean, all this time—'

'Mr Kellerman wouldn't let Jim take the blame and maybe
be arrested. He was ill, you see—Jim, I mean—he'd had a
serious heart condition for years. Then when Philip—he was
our son—when he committed suicide I think Jim went a little
out of his mind.'

Kate hesitated. 'I believe your son was infatuated with Mrs
Kellerman,' she ventured, and Mrs Muir didn't seem surprised to hear that she knew that, too.

'He was,' she said bitterly, 'but she was only playing with
him. Even when she was expecting his child, she told him
to get out of her life.'

Kate breathed deeply. 'And Alex—I mean, Mr
Kellerman—told you not to say anything?'

'That's right. Jim confessed what he'd done to Mr
Kellerman. Jim and I have worked here all our lives, and
we've known Alex since he was a little boy. He and Philip
used to play together when they were children. They were
such good friends. I think that's why Pamela—Mrs
Kellerman—tried to split them up.

'Anyway, as I say, Jim was sick, and we all knew he'd
never survive being charged with such a serious offence. That
was when Mr Kellerman said that we should say nothing.
There was no proof that anyone had done it deliberately and
I'm afraid we let Mr Kellerman take the blame.'

'Oh, Mrs Muir!'

'I know.' The housekeeper looked pale and defeated. 'And
you're the first person, other than Mr Kellerman, that I've

told the story to. At least Jim had several more months of comparative freedom. Though I don't think he ever forgave himself for the abuse Mr Kellerman had to suffer because of what he'd done.'

Or the anguish, thought Kate, with feeling. Alex had lost his wife and had been in danger of losing his livelihood too. Had he thought of Rachel, when he'd made that quixotic decision to shoulder the burden? Had he realised that Conrad Wyatt would use the situation to his own selfish ends?

She thought not. Which probably explained why he'd taken it so badly when the truth hit him. She thought in his position she might have felt like hitting the bottle, too. There'd been no turning back, even though Jim Muir had died only months after the accident. Kate sighed. Poor Alex. No wonder he'd become so bitter. He'd lost his wife and his child for a crime he didn't commit.

Kate shrugged her shoulders now. 'I don't know what to say.'

'Don't say anything.' Mrs Muir put her tissue away again and picked up her bag. 'I just didn't want you to go on believing that Mr Kellerman had killed his wife.'

'I never believed that.' As Kate said the words she realised she meant them.

'You didn't?' Mrs Muir looked confused. 'But I understood you'd told Mrs Sheridan that that was why you took the job.'

'No.' Kate was horrified. Lacey Sheridan had found a way to get her revenge, after all. 'I told Alex Alicia was missing and I agreed to try and find her. I had no preconceptions about how Pamela had died before I came to Jamaica Hill. And—and once I'd met Mr Kellerman I knew instinctively that he'd had nothing to do with his wife's death.'

'Do you mean that?' There were tears shining in Mrs Muir's eyes now, and Kate nodded.

'Of course I mean it. And—and I hope you'll tell Alex what I said. I—I know he and Lacey are very close, and he's more likely to believe her than me, but I'd like to feel that he won't think too badly of me when I'm gone.'

'When you're gone?'

Mrs Muir looked puzzled now, and Kate wished she hadn't spoken so impulsively. 'Yes,' she said at last. 'I'm giving up the agency and moving to London in a few weeks. I'm hoping to get a chance to work as a solicitor. I have a law degree, but I've never been able to find a firm in King's Montford willing to take me on.'

'And—and will your daughter be going with you?'

'Of course.' Kate forced a smile. 'And my mother, too. She's not very keen at the moment, but it will be good for Joanne to have a fresh start at a new school. She's been having some problems at Lady Montford so I don't think she'll mind.'

'You do know Rachel's living at Jamaica Hill again,' ventured the housekeeper suddenly, and Kate felt a glow of warmth at the thought that she had played a small part in her return.

'No, I didn't,' she said. 'But I'm happy for—for both of them. I suppose Alex feels he's getting his life back together again.'

'Well, yes.' Mrs Muir looked down at her hands gripping her bag. 'People have been so sympathetic. I think some of them have been having second thoughts since Conrad Wyatt was arrested, and the stables have never been busier. Of course, there's still to be a hearing about Rachel's future, but the authorities seem to think that it's just a formality. She belongs with her father. And Jamaica Hill needs a family again.'

And it's going to get one, thought Kate, somewhat jealously. Though she doubted Lacey was the kind of woman to appreciate having a four-year-old stepchild thrust upon her. As for Rachel herself—well, Kate supposed she always had Mrs Muir to turn to. The old housekeeper would always be there for her, even when her father went away.

Mrs Muir got to her feet. 'I suppose I'd better be going.'

'Yes.' Kate rose, too. 'But thank you for coming, and trusting me with the truth. I'm honoured that you felt you could tell me the whole story. I hope you'll all be very happy in the future.'

Susie came back into Kate's office after showing Mrs Muir out, her eyes wide and curious. 'What did she want?' she asked, and Kate sighed and sank back into her chair.

'She wanted to thank me,' she said. 'For finding Alicia. Now, will you take those revolting doughnuts away before I throw up?'

Susie left for home about five o'clock, as usual. The office was quiet after she'd left, and Kate knew there was no point in her hanging around either. There was only a week to go, a week until she handed over the lease to her landlord. Her mother thought she was crazy, but then, her mother didn't know all the facts.

Nevertheless, she hoped that one of the jobs she'd applied for proved suitable. Even though her father's sister, Aunt Bridget, had said she could stay with her while she was looking for accommodation, money was still going to be tight. Of course, when they sold the flat they'd have a little capital to put down on another property, but Kate had already accepted that it might not be as nice as what they had now.

Which wasn't saying a lot, she thought glumly. When they'd first moved into the flat in Milner Court, they'd all missed the garden they used to have at the house. And now she was expecting her mother to move again, into even less salubrious surroundings. Was she being selfish? Wouldn't it just be easier to speak to Alex and let him play his part?

No!

The idea of asking Alex for anything had evaporated as soon as she'd contemplated Lacey's reaction to what she had to tell him. The thought of Lacey Sheridan making mocking comments about her naïvety was humiliating. She couldn't expose herself to the other woman's pity or contempt.

So—they had to move away from King's Montford. And

as London seemed like the only place where she might be able to pick up her career she had no choice in the matter. It would be good for Joanne, she told herself firmly. Even if the thought of an inner-city comprehensive filled her with dismay.

It was cold in the office, and she turned to close the window. She'd opened it a crack to allow the smell of Susie's perfume to escape, and now the frosty air was chilling the room. But these days anything—strongly smelling food, disinfectants, perfume—they all affected her stomach. She was seriously thinking of going to the doctor for some pills to calm her down.

The door slammed in the outer office, and she turned abruptly, her heart beating rapidly at the thought that someone might have come in. Unless her closing the window had caused a backdraught, she considered hopefully. The office was closed, the sign had been taken down; and, in any case, they'd always closed at five o'clock.

Her heart almost stopped beating altogether when she heard a footstep. Someone was in Susie's office, and she wondered if her assistant had forgotten something and come back to fetch it. 'Susie?' she called faintly, realising she sounded as nervous as she felt. 'Susie, is that you?'

The silhouette in the half-glassed door was definitely not female, and she was horribly reminded of the kind of friends Henry Sawyer might have. He certainly had cause to feel resentful towards her. Because of her evidence, he was facing charges as well.

She stood motionless behind her chair, gripping the back with nervous fingers as her door opened. Then her knees almost gave out on her completely when she saw who it was. 'Alex!' she exclaimed weakly. 'I mean—Mr Kellerman,' she corrected herself. 'Oh, you frightened me.' She struggled to gather her scattered wits. 'I didn't know who was there.'

'And now you do,' said Alex, coming into the office and closing the door. 'So this is where you work.' He looked about him as he unzipped his black leather blouson jacket.

Underneath he was wearing a dark blue silk shirt that complemented his swarthy colouring. 'Or should I say *worked*? Agnes tells me you're leaving town.'

Kate swallowed, averting her eyes from his lean, muscled torso. 'Um—what do you want?' she asked tautly, wishing she'd known it was him before he opened the door. As it was, she had had no time to prepare herself. He looked so good, so disturbing, so just as she remembered him. Did he realise how cruel it was to torment her? No, of course not. Mrs Muir had delivered the news that she was closing the office, and he'd decided she deserved a personal goodbye.

'A loaded question,' he remarked now, lounging into the chair his housekeeper had occupied earlier. He crossed one booted foot across his knee and rested one hand on his thigh. The other curled around the arm of the chair, smoothing the wood almost sensuously. Kate thought of those hands caressing her body. Could she bear the thought that he might never touch her again?

She doubted it.

'Why are you leaving town?' he asked abruptly, when she didn't make any comment. 'Has somebody said something, or done something, to make you feel you can't live here any more?'

Only you...

'If there have been any threats...' he continued, and she realised he'd no idea why she was leaving. 'Kate.' He thrust one hand through his hair in a frustrated gesture. 'For God's sake, answer me, can't you? Don't I at least deserve to know what's going on?'

No...

Kate sighed, and, feeling her way round the chair, almost like an old woman, she sank bonelessly into the seat. 'It's— it's this business,' she said. 'It's going nowhere.' Which was true. 'I've decided to try and put my degree to some use, after all.'

'Where?'

'Does it matter?'

'Humour me,' he said, a muscle jumping in his jaw.

'Well—' Kate paused. 'We're probably going to live in London. I've applied for a couple of vacancies, and I've got an interview for one of them next week.'

'Don't go.'

His request was delivered with clipped intensity, and Kate was glad she was sitting down when she looked into his hard face. 'I don't have any choice,' she said, trying to speak lightly. 'Um—Mrs Muir says you've got Rachel back again. I'm so happy for you both.'

'Are you?'

'Well, of course.' Kate couldn't bear his hostile expression and she hurried on, 'I know nothing can justify what I did in your eyes, but at least the outcome wasn't bad. I should have realised sooner that Conrad Wyatt was involved. If I'd had the sense to look into Henry Sawyer's background, I might have discovered he'd worked for the Wyatts in the past.'

'You didn't know.'

Alex's tone was flat and accepting, but Kate had to make her confession. 'But I should have done,' she said. 'That— that's one of the reasons why I'm giving up the agency. I've discovered I'm not very good at this job. A more experienced investigator would have had their suspicions right from the start.'

'Don't beat yourself up over it.' Alex shrugged indifferently. 'No one could have imagined how devious Conrad would prove to be. Perhaps it was my fault. Perhaps I should have seen how Pam's death had affected him and tried harder to gain his sympathy. My wife's death was a tragic accident. I think he thought that I didn't care.'

'Because you let him believe that you didn't know who'd put the horses in different stalls,' said Kate quietly, and Alex frowned.

'What did you say?' he asked, but she knew he had heard her anyway.

'Mrs Muir told me,' she admitted, feeling the colour warming her pale cheeks. 'She told me about her husband—and her son.'

Alex's nostrils flared. 'Oh, did she?'

'Yes.'

'And what else did she tell you that I should know about? I assume you discussed the case as well.'

'Only briefly.' Kate gripped the edge of the desk. 'I still don't know all the details myself, so I could hardly discuss the case with her.'

'But you know Wyatt was arrested and charged, and released on bail pending the trial? You know it was Sawyer who threw Alicia's suitcases into the skip?'

'No.' Kate tried to stop watching him so greedily. But, God knew, this might be the last chance she'd have to imprint his image in her mind. 'So—so why did they do it? Surely the fact that Alicia was missing was enough.'

'Hardly.' Alex looked as if he would have preferred to talk about other things, but he evidently decided to humour her. 'Things weren't developing fast enough, even though they had gone to the expense of hiring you. You see,' he sighed, 'I think they assumed reporting Alicia's disappearance to the police would promote some kind of investigation. Then they could alert the media to what was going on, and the whole circus would begin again.'

'You mean like—when Pamela died?'

'That's right.' Alex was laconic. 'But people go missing every day, and the police simply don't have the resources to follow up every lead.' He paused. 'I guess that's why they hired you; they hoped you'd be convinced and report your findings to the authorities. But you didn't, so they had to think of something else.'

'Hence the suitcases.' Kate shook her head disbelievingly.

'Well, it was a fairly damning piece of evidence, you have to admit.' Alex grimaced. 'And with Inspector Rivers on my case, desperate to prove he was a better detective than his predecessor, they might have succeeded. Sufficiently so to create doubts in people's minds, at least.'

'And Alicia?'

'What about her?'

'Why did she do it?'

Alex shrugged. 'Who knows? For the money, I suppose.'

'But Henry Sawyer said you'd given her a room at your house.'

'I did.' Alex heaved another sigh. 'She fed me some story that her husband used to beat her, just after she came to work for me. She persuaded me that she was desperate. That she needed somewhere to stay temporarily until she could find a place of her own.'

'I see.'

'I did not have an affair with her, if that's what you're wondering,' he said harshly. 'Despite what you may have heard to the contrary.'

'Not least, from you,' murmured Kate, remembering that awful day at the stables' office, and Alex stared at her with uncomprehending eyes.

'The day—the day you found out who I really was,' she prompted reluctantly, and Alex's expression cleared as he remembered what she meant.

'I was angry that day,' he muttered. 'Bloody angry. I'd thought—well, it doesn't matter what I'd thought now. The fact was, I thought I was in deep trouble and you were a part of it.'

'I wasn't.'

'I know that now. I think I realised it as soon as I saw your face. But I didn't want to let you off too easily. And when that supercilious inspector appeared I'd have said anything to destroy your relief.'

Kate bent her head. 'Well, you certainly did that. I thought you were going to go charging off to see Conrad Wyatt. I worried about it all morning, and then, when I looked at Alicia's picture again...'

'Yeah.' Alex blew out a breath. 'Well, I didn't. And I never thanked you for finding Alicia, when I should have done. But, after what Lacey told me, I guessed you wouldn't want anything from me. That was why I had Julian write that letter.' He grimaced. 'A formal note of thanks for saving my life.'

Kate pressed her hands down on the desk and got to her feet. 'I didn't save your life,' she protested. 'And—and I don't know what Lacey—that is, Mrs Sheridan—told you, but I don't think it was anything I'd said.' She breathed deeply. 'If she told you I only took the job because I was convinced you were guilty of your wife's murder, I have to tell you she was—wasn't telling the truth.'

'You mean, she was lying?'

He looked up at her through narrowed lids, and Kate knew her control was wavering. If he didn't get out of here soon, she had the feeling she was going to start to scream. Why couldn't he just go? Why didn't he see that by staying he was just labouring the situation? She now knew that he and Lacey were together. Wasn't that enough?

Shaking her head, she turned away towards the window. 'Mrs Muir probably got it wrong,' she said. 'Mrs Sheridan doesn't even know me.'

'But she came to see you, didn't she? That day you were leaving?' he queried. 'Sam Guthrie said he saw her leaving the office just after your daughter went in.'

'All right.' Kate couldn't hold out any longer. 'She came to tell me that—that you and she—'

'Had slept together a few times?' suggested Alex flatly, and when she glanced over her shoulder she saw that he had risen to his feet as well.

'That you were lovers,' she amended tightly, turning back to the rain-smeared window. 'It's all right. You don't owe me any explanation—'

'Dammit, it's not all right,' he snarled angrily. She heard him shove the chair he had been sitting on aside, and presently she felt the heat of his body at her back. 'There was no love between Lace and me,' he contradicted. 'Though I'm not denying that she offered me some comfort when I needed it. It's not conceit to say that she got as much out of it as me.'

Kate was shaking her head again. 'Like I said, it's nothing to do with me—'

'And if I want to make it your concern?' he demanded harshly. 'What then?'

'What do you mean?' Much against her better judgement, she turned to face him. 'You don't need my permission for who you take to bed.'

He was close, so close, and the urge to touch him was almost overwhelming. She wondered, if he had any feelings for her, why he didn't touch her. Instead, he just stood looking down at her, at the unmistakable hardening of her nipples. And although she wanted to reach out to him she kept her arms anchored to her sides.

'I took you to bed, remember?' he said at last, huskily, the warm draught of his breath fanning her feathering skin. 'Well, not actually bed, but your sofa was quite comfortable. I'd never had an experience that good before.'

Kate felt as if the air in the room was getting thinner. It was becoming difficult to drag sufficient oxygen into her straining lungs. She couldn't meet his eyes, so she concentrated on his open collar, on the shadow of dark hair she could see outlined beneath his shirt.

'I'm sure you must have,' she said at last, when she could speak coherently. 'And—and now that you've got Rachel back you can think about the future again. I'm sure Mrs Sheridan will learn to love your daughter—'

'God!' He swore then, and his hands fastened on her shoulders. 'Listen to me,' he told her grimly, 'I don't care if Lacey could learn to love Rachel or not.' His thumbs tilted her chin so that she was forced to look up at him. 'Lacey has no part in my future, do you hear me? I may not even have a future if you walk out on me now.'

Kate quivered. 'You don't mean that.'

'And if I do? Would it matter to you then?'

'It matters.' But Kate backed away from his hands, not

daring to believe what she was hearing. 'I just don't know what you want from me. You said—you said that what we had was just—sex.'

'Yeah, I know. I said a lot of things. And I'm not denying that I've fought against admitting what I feel for you.' He groaned. 'But, dammit, when Agnes said you were leaving, I knew I couldn't let you do it. Not without seeing you; not without speaking to you again. Not without giving myself the chance to find out if what Lace had said was true.'

'It's not.' Kate trembled. 'I think she knew how I felt about you—'

'Which is?'

His eyes burned into hers, and she moved her head from side to side, trying to find the words to meet his need. 'Well—that I love you, I suppose,' she said defeatedly, and he made a sound of triumph as he moved towards her.

'You love me,' he said, lifting his hands and smoothing his thumbs over the dark shadows beneath her eyes. 'Is that why you haven't been sleeping properly? Why you've got such an air of fragility?'

Kate found it hard to answer that. 'I suppose so,' she breathed, her words stifled by the brush of his mouth. Her hands curled convulsively about his shoulders. 'Do you love me?'

'Is there any doubt?' he demanded, his voice breaking with emotion. 'Hell, Kate, of course I love you. But I thought— well, that Lace was right. That you had just been playing me along for the sake of your investigations; and besides, what decent woman would want a barely reformed character like me?'

'I would.' Gaining in confidence, Kate wound her arms around his neck. 'Oh, Alex! I don't know what to say. Are you sure about this?'

'As sure as I've ever been in my life,' he muttered fiercely. 'What I can't understand is, why were you going to leave without giving me a chance to make amends?'

EPILOGUE

'I HAVE to admit, it is much more comfortable here,' murmured Alex, some two hours later, rolling onto his side and gazing down possessively at the woman to whom he'd just made slow, sensuous love. Flushed among the tumbled covers of his bed, Kate had never looked more desirable, and he thought how amazing it was that even though he'd taken her twice already he wanted her again.

'Is this really your room?' she asked, deliciously uninhibited in the way she didn't object when he bent to suckle one provocatively swollen breast. 'Mmm, that's nice.' Her breath caught in her throat. 'Oh, Alex, do that again.'

'I intend to,' he said thickly, but then he forced himself to draw back. There was still so much they had to say to one another, and he still nurtured anxieties as to why she would choose to leave King's Montford rather than wait to see if what Lacey had implied was true.

He was not incognizant of the fact that she had avoided any personal questions at her office, choosing instead to indulge in the kind of heavy petting that had left him hard and aching, and mindless with need. Then she'd insisted on calling her mother and explaining that she was spending the evening with him, without ever mentioning the fact that they loved one another.

Why?

His stomach clenched unpleasantly. In God's name, surely she had no doubts about him now?

As if she'd detected his uncertainty, Kate chose that moment to reach up and bestow a lingering kiss at the corner of his mouth, and for a moment Alex allowed his senses to spin wildly out of control. It was so easy to give in to emotion, to forget about tomorrow. But he loved her. He wanted to know what she wasn't telling him.

As it was, he'd had to wait until Rachel was safely tucked in bed before they could be alone together. The little girl had been so excited to see Kate again, and she'd insisted on wringing a promise from her that Kate would bring Joanne to see her tomorrow.

Which was another reason why he wanted to know what Kate was thinking. Rachel had been hurt too many times already. He couldn't take the risk that she might be hurt again.

And although Kate protested when he drew back he wouldn't allow her to sway his mood. 'We have to talk,' he said, sitting up so that he could look down at her. 'It's important.'

'I know.' Despite his fears, there was only tenderness in Kate's eyes, and he was sorely tempted to leave all their talking until later. Much later.

'This room will have to be decorated,' she said, before he could formulate his questions. 'Perhaps green and gold? Do you like green and gold? I do.'

'This isn't the master bedroom,' said Alex mechanically, wondering if he was ever going to get a straight answer from her. 'You can choose which suite we use when you move in here.' He paused. 'I'm assuming you do want to move in here. You and Joanne—and your mother, too, if she's agreeable. There's plenty of room. She could have an apartment all to herself.'

A frown marred Kate's smooth forehead now. 'You're not still having doubts about my feelings?' she asked faintly. She swallowed. 'Or perhaps you're having doubts about your own?'

'Don't be stupid!' Alex was harsh, but he couldn't help it. 'I'm crazy about you, you know that. I want to marry you, for God's sake!' He groaned. 'I just can't get my head round why you were planning on going away.'

Kate hesitated, and then she scrambled up to sit cross-legged beside him. But this time she tucked the quilt beneath her arms, as if she knew how her naked body made him feel. 'What else could I do?' she asked softly. 'I—I'm pregnant. I didn't want you to feel—trapped—because I was having your child.'

Alex stared at her, open-mouthed, trying to make some sense of what she was saying. 'You're pregnant?' he echoed weakly. 'My God, why didn't you tell me before?'

'Before what?' Kate gazed at him gently. 'Before I made arrangements to leave King's Montford, or before I knew you loved me?' She touched his hand with loving fingers. 'Do you mind?'

'God—' Alex cast the covers aside and reached eagerly for her. 'How could I mind? It's as much my doing as yours.' His smile was brilliant. 'And I was thinking that perhaps you thought I was being too impatient. That you needed more time to decide what you really wanted to do.'

'Oh, I know what I want to do,' Kate assured him firmly as he bore her back against the pillows and covered her mouth with his. 'It just seemed like a dream, the kind of dream that could never happen. Loving you, living with you, having your child…'

It was some little time before Alex recovered himself sufficiently to talk practicalities. 'Do you think Joanne will object when she hears she's not going to leave Lady Montford after all?'

'What? When she's going to live here with all these horses?' Kate shook her head positively. 'Besides, my mother will be pleased. She always says there's nothing to be gained by running away.'

'Isn't that the truth?' Alex stroked the moist hair back from her forehead. 'What about your mother? Do you think she'll accept me as her son-in-law after all this?'

'My mother's a fairly generous woman. And I know when she hears about the baby she'll be thrilled. As for Joanne, well—she thinks you're pretty terrific. She's probably going to be the least surprised of us all.'

'Smart girl.' Alex grinned. 'So we're going to have three children?'

'To begin with,' said Kate provocatively, putting out her tongue. Then she sobered, running her nail over the beard that was roughening his jawline. 'What about Rachel? Is this going to be very hard for her?'

'Maybe I'm being selfish, but I think it's exactly what Rachel is needing,' declared Alex, grasping her hand and taking her fingers to his mouth. 'A normal home, a normal family, a new baby.' He grimaced. 'I can even find it in my heart to pity Wyatt after this.'

Kate nodded. 'I suppose I feel sorry for him. Well, his wife, anyway. I don't suppose she did anything wrong.'

'Except condone her husband's actions,' said Alex wryly. 'But, knowing Conrad as I do, I doubt she had a choice.'

'Will you let them see Rachel again?'

'Of course. Eventually.' Alex gave a heavy sigh and rolled onto his back. 'And now, I suppose, we ought to go and tell your mother and Joanne.' He grinned. 'I wonder if I'll feel old if Joanne calls me Dad...?'

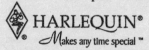

If you enjoyed what you just read,
then we've got an offer you can't resist!

Take 2 bestselling love stories FREE!

Plus get a FREE surprise gift!

Clip this page and mail it to Harlequin Reader Service®

IN U.S.A.	**IN CANADA**
3010 Walden Ave.	P.O. Box 609
P.O. Box 1867	Fort Erie, Ontario
Buffalo, N.Y. 14240-1867	L2A 5X3

YES! Please send me 2 free Harlequin Presents® novels and my free surprise gift. Then send me 6 brand-new novels every month, which I will receive months before they're available in stores. In the U.S.A., bill me at the bargain price of $3.12 plus 25¢ delivery per book and applicable sales tax, if any*. In Canada, bill me at the bargain price of $3.49 plus 25¢ delivery per book and applicable taxes**. That's the complete price and a savings of over 10% off the cover prices—what a great deal! I understand that accepting the 2 free books and gift places me under no obligation ever to buy any books. I can always return a shipment and cancel at any time. Even if I never buy another book from Harlequin, the 2 free books and gift are mine to keep forever. So why not take us up on our invitation. You'll be glad you did!

106 HEN CNER
306 HEN CNES

Name	(PLEASE PRINT)
Address	Apt.#
City	State/Prov.	Zip/Postal Code

* Terms and prices subject to change without notice. Sales tax applicable in N.Y.
** Canadian residents will be charged applicable provincial taxes and GST.
All orders subject to approval. Offer limited to one per household.
® are registered trademarks of Harlequin Enterprises Limited.

PRES99   ©1998 Harlequin Enterprises Limited

HARLEQUIN ◆ PRESENTS®

Wedded Bliss

Penny Jordan Carole Mortimer

Two brand-new stories—for the price of one!—
in one easy-to-read volume.
Especially written by your favorite authors!

Wedded Bliss
Harlequin Presents #2031, June 1999
THEY'RE WED AGAIN!
by Penny Jordan
and
THE MAN SHE'LL MARRY
by Carole Mortimer

There's nothing more exciting than a wedding!
Share the excitement as two couples make their very
different journeys which will take them up the aisle to
embark upon a life of happiness!

Available **next month** wherever Harlequin books
are sold.

HARLEQUIN®
Makes any time special ™

Look us up on-line at: http://www.romance.net   HP2IN1

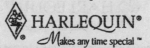

Coming Next Month

HARLEQUIN PRESENTS®

THE BEST HAS JUST GOTTEN BETTER!

#2037 THE SPANISH GROOM Lynne Graham
To please his ailing godfather, Cesar Valverde agreed to marry
Dixie Robinson. Unexpectedly, he found her to be an achingly
sensual woman. So within a week, his fake fiancée had
become his wife and become pregnant!

#2038 THE SECRET MISTRESS Emma Darcy
Presents Passion
Luis Martinez had never forgiven Shontelle for walking away
from their affair. But now she needed his help, and Luis saw a
way to exact vengeance for his wounded pride: he'd keep her
safe in exchange for one night in her bed...

#2039 TO WOO A WIFE Carole Mortimer
Bachelor Brothers
As a beautiful, young widow, Abbie was wary of emotional
and physical involvement. Jarrett was used to being a winner
in the boardroom and the bedroom, so to him, Abbie was the
ultimate challenge: she needed wooing!

#2040 HE'S MY HUSBAND! Lindsay Armstrong
Nicola was Brett's wife of convenience, but it seemed to
her that he had other admirers. Nicola loved Brett and his
children, so the time had come to show everyone, including
Brett, exactly whose husband he really was!

#2041 THE UNEXPECTED BABY Diana Hamilton
Expecting!
Elena was deeply in love with her brand-new husband, Jed, so
discovering she was pregnant should have completed her joy.
Elena knew she'd have to tell Jed, but would their marriage
survive the truth?

#2042 REMARRIED IN HASTE Sandra Field
Brant Curtis had dreamed about his ex-wife, Rowan, for years,
and now he was face-to-face with her. He didn't have a plan,
but he wanted more than a one night stand for old times'
sake—he wanted his wife back, whatever it took!